HUNT FOR THE SHEPHERD

SUSAN BENNETT

First published in paperback by
Michael Terence Publishing in 2023
www.mtp.agency

ISBN 9781800946873

This book is dedicated to a wonderful son-in-law, Jake Medler who lost his life so tragically, and unexpectedly, at the age of thirty-six.

He was always very enthusiastic and encouraging about this novel, and because he features as one of the characters, I believe that his memory will never fade.

In the words of Shakespeare's Sonnet 18,

So long as men can breathe or eyes can see,
So long lives this, and this gives life to thee.

One

Sunday 9th December 2018

A bright, but chilly start to a December morning suggested the promise of a pleasant day ahead. Yet by lunchtime, the once crystal blue sky had decayed to a pallor of wishy-washy grey, that grew darker and angrier by the hour and bared down on the Earth threatening to deliver a downpour. By twilight, the threat was realised, and one of the dirtiest nights of the year was unleashed upon them.

The relentless onslaught of a wintry squall sought out and infiltrated, even the smallest of gaps in their clothing. Drenched, and at the mercy of the elements, they knew they'd drawn the short straw, but someone had to do it. Someone had to step up to the plate because you can't stop trains in an instant, it takes time to organise. Accordingly, until it was safe to walk the track, hacking a path through the dense thicket, was the only option in their search for a body, that reportedly lay beside it.

Being the first responders, their equipment was literally whatever they had in the boot of their cars, and for the most part, it was woefully inadequate for the requirements of the task. Nevertheless, they persevered, hoping the person may be found alive. But where was the body? Evidently, the stretch of the track chosen for the search, had been determined based on an observation from a passenger on a moving train. He thought it was a minute or two after he saw the body, that the train pulled into Norwood Junction station, where he alighted and raised the alarm. Consequently, since the scene had not been definitively identified, they were in essence, thrashing about in the dark hoping to stumble across it.

At the outset, three possible scenarios were considered. Firstly, it could be a poor misguided soul, who thought it was a good idea to try and cross the track, perhaps as a short cut home. Secondly, it could be the victim of an assault, but that idea held little credence. After all, it was hard enough for them to reach trackside, let alone someone having to negotiate the brambles and drag a body too. Thirdly, and the most favoured, is a person who has trodden the suicide path. Whichever it turned out to be, the hope was that they would reach them in time and a life would be saved, but in the main, the expectation was that the person would be found deceased. In that event, a further expectation was that there would be body parts to find and recover, hence, the supply of triple-layer face masks, and biological collection bags to all team members involved in the search.

On the road parallel to the track, four squad cars had positioned themselves strategically to isolate the designated area from traffic and the public. It was imperative that the scene should be kept away from prying eyes and preserved as much as possible. Nobody knew how long the victim had laid there, and regardless of the circumstances, it would be crucial to collect forensic material. But the rotten weather was their enemy, and no doubt the rain would have washed away most of any evidence by now.

A further team of officers, a couple of paramedics, and DI Spence from CID had assembled at the end of platform one. All were eager to get searching, but the tracks were the domain of the railway and Network Rail's Mobile Operations Manager. Before they could examine the closed section of the track, they all had to receive a briefing on rail safety, don Hi-Vis safety wear, and be issued with super bright flashlight torches. The question though, on everyone's lips was why? Why was CID involved in what was expected to be a recovery operation?

Were there suspicious circumstances? Do they have an idea who it may be? The questions were to remain unanswered as DI Spence kept his usual tight-lipped.

19:15

It was now seven-fifteen, the shift change was well underway at the station, and with it came the questions.

"Where's DI Spence?" demanded an aggravated colleague. He was eager to get home and needed to deliver his feedback on his eventful shift.

"I need to hand over. Where the hell is he?" he called out.

No reply was forthcoming from the officers assembled, just a Mexican wave of shrugging shoulders indicated they were all in the dark as to his whereabouts.

"He's on his way. I've just seen him parking up," came a voice from the corridor.

All heads turned to see who was speaking, and as the face appeared in the doorway, a spontaneous roar went up! It was DC Michael Harris - he was back!

To those who didn't know him, they saw a lanky policeman, with a pale complexion, a fade haircut, and big ears. To those who did, they saw a man in recovery and a shadow of his former self.

The outpouring of affection, the handshaking and back-slapping by his colleagues, was unexpected and left him feeling a little embarrassed. However, his awkwardness was quick to dissipate with the entrance of Spence, who, as expected, made a B-line for him, and with a hefty clout to his arm, duly pronounced that the dream team were now fully reassembled.

As the exuberant atmosphere ebbed away, Spence went off to do his handover, and normal working in the CID office resumed. Harris was more than pleased to get stuck into a tray of paperwork, his thoughts would then be focused on the job at hand, instead of reliving painful memories.

It had been almost five months since he was signed off work after suffering a mental breakdown. A devastating blow to his career prospects and caused entirely by the trauma he experienced while investigating, identifying, and trapping a homicidal psychopath. All the officers on the task force were affected in one way or another, but Harris had also experienced the shock of realising that he didn't possess the inner strength he always believed he had. He wasn't resilient. He couldn't assimilate, repair, and return to work like the others, and for a while, his mental health spiralled out of control. It took the intervention by Spence, his compassion, his inspiring and encouraging approach, and of course, his money for the treatment, to bring about Harris' recovery.

Known as the rock of the department, DI Jack Spence is dependable, reliable, and hard when he needs to be. He is a well-built, tall, broad-shouldered man, and can often appear intimidating to the newly acquainted. He believes in policing by the book, doesn't suffer fools, is tenacious in pursuit of the truth, and is widely considered to be a superb mentor to new recruits. But Harris seemed to bring out the paternal instinct in him. He was the son he always wanted and didn't hesitate in coming forward to help. And now, after months of therapy, Harris was feeling positive about his future. He'd dispensed with the anti-depressants and believed himself ready to enter the world of work again. So too Spence. He was elated to have his lad back on board and convinced it would be business as usual. However, not everyone shared in his optimism. One officer in particular, who held strong reservations about Harris' return to normal duties, was DCI Dave Fielding.

Heading up CID for five eventful, and successful years, Fielding was a highly respected officer by all at the station, but especially, by the top brass. Latterly, he'd been instrumental in the capture, and subsequent conviction of several high-profile villains, and was expecting to receive a promotion as a result. But as it stands, he remains in post. It seems that nothing is ever straightforward in CID, so only time will tell about the movement of personnel, and who does what.

Today, he too was on the evening shift, and popping his head around the main office door, called out, "Evening everyone."

With a flurry of heads, came severally replies, "Evening sir."

Then focusing his attention on Harris, asked, "When DI Spence is finished, ask him to come to my office please," then seemingly as an afterthought, added, "nice to see you back Harris."

"Thank you, sir." came the tepid reply.

So unlike Harris. He was always seen as a carbon copy of Spence, with a loud, resonating voice, and the excitable personality of a puppy. Was he still adjusting to his return, or was his return too early, as some now suspected?

Fielding's pained expression at his response left nothing to the imagination. And instead of striding off as is usually the case, he lingered by the door, making small talk with anyone passing, and surreptitiously, or so he thought, checked back to observe him. It was an uncomfortable few minutes for all in the office, and everyone, bar Harris, who had kept his head down the entire time, was relieved when Spence appeared, and the two men walked off to Fielding's office.

Fielding asked Spence to close the door behind him, a clear sign that something private was about to be discussed.

"Well Jack, was it her?"

Spence shook his head. "No, thank God."

That out of the way, Spence moved to a chair at the side of the desk, and Fielding sat behind it.

Although relieved that it wasn't his niece and that he wouldn't be making that awful call to his sister, Spence was feeling angry. He knew it was unreasonable to be angry but couldn't help the way he felt.

"Bloody kid. Her mum and dad are frantic with worry. All she has to do is make a bloody phone call. That's not too much to ask, is it?"

"What made you think it could be your niece on the tracks?"

"Nothing, but I've got no choice other than to check all, and every account of bodies found. I know her mental health is an issue, and my sister believes she could be suicidal."

Fielding shook his head in sadness at the thought of someone in her teens being so mentally fragile. Then opening a folder that lay on the desk, asked,

"Whilst we're on the subject of mental health. Are you sure about Harris?"

"Yes, he's been cleared as fit for work. We just need to give him time to readjust."

Fielding seemed unconvinced, but these two men had known and worked together for many years, and he had no reason not to trust Spence's judgement now.

"Okay. Just keep me informed of any worries or concerns you may have."

"I will, but I don't anticipate any. The lad will be fine," he replied bullishly.

The air now cleared, and it was down to business.

"Do we know who the victim is?" asked Fielding.

Spence shook his head, "No ID was found. All I can tell you at this stage is that it's a young girl."

"And is there any reason to suspect foul play?"

"I doubt it. Uniform is dealing with it. If anything seems suspicious, they'll be in touch. I expect it will be a suicide, but we'll have to wait for the pathologist's report to confirm it. Poor lass."

Two

Monday 10th December – 07:00

Following a call from the pathologist in the early hours, which made clear that the tragic death of this young girl was murder, Spence had been in conversation with Fielding, and wasted no time in getting to the station. The post-mortem summary had already been hand delivered and given to Fielding as the senior investigating officer. A second copy for Spence's eyes lay on his desk.

As he opened the buff folder, he remembered his first sight of her on the track, and how his pulse raced at the thought it could be his niece lying there in the rain. It had been a dark and dirty night, and the persistent, icy drizzle had played tricks with the lamplight. All he could make out in the distance was her short blonde hair. His niece had short blonde hair. His heart was in his mouth as he rounded on the body, and still cannot find the words to express his relief when he realised that her hair, was where the resemblance ended. His niece was a good deal taller, and significantly bigger built than this young victim. Solemnly, he read the information, it was heart-breaking.

It identified a female, fourteen to sixteen years old. The cause of death was not due to colliding with a train but the result of an overdose of the opiate Fentanyl, and concluded that on administration of the drug, her death would have been instantaneous. The time of death was determined to be approximately forty-eight hours before her body was discovered, and as no drug paraphernalia was found with the body, the victim must have died elsewhere and subsequently been dumped at the tracks.

On inspection, the injection site for the fatal dose was identified, and the person responsible for administering it, is considered to have some medical knowledge, or perhaps be a skilful drug user; the injection being described as intramuscular (IM), one that is given deep into the muscle where the drug can be absorbed quickly. No other injection sites were found on her body, and the absence of metabolites in her hair follicles, confirmed she was not a drug user.

Scarring and recent lacerations were identified on her inner arms, suggesting long-term and sustained self-harming, and she was also considered to be underweight for her age; the subsequent identification of muscle wastage, along with dry, inelastic skin, confirmed the suspicion of malnutrition.

The examination also found her to be sexually active, with evidence of bruising around the vaginal area. This, along with bruising around her wrists, would suggest she had been restrained and subjected to a sexual assault. However, it could also be attributed to rough sex; a possibility if she had been engaged in prostitution. STD testing established the presence of Chlamydia, and although semen was also recovered, the donor remains unidentified but was confirmed as a white male. She did not have any distinguishing marks or tattoos.

Accompanying the PM was a drawn image of the body position when it was found, and an itemised record of the clothing and accessories present. She was wearing age twelve to thirteen, light blue jeans, that were ripped at the knees, the waist button unfastened, the zip undone. Any maker's labels had been removed. And an age twelve to thirteen white cotton blouse, with a narrow collar and buttoned down the front. The top button was missing, and the image of a small, plain, white button, was attached. Any maker's labels had been removed. It was also recorded that her nails had been French manicured recently. She was not wearing any footwear, underwear, or jewellery.

09:45

Fielding had set the investigation wheels in motion immediately, and Spence had assembled the team for their first briefing. Everyone had been given the opportunity to make a preliminary start on their assignments, and time to read the summary reports before the briefing began. They were particularly requested to write down their thoughts. It was the way Fielding liked to work. He agreed with brainstorming but liked it to have an element of thoughtfulness and organisation. The whole idea of people coming up with things spontaneously, he found annoying. In his experience, when people hadn't had the time to think it through, he'd wasted valuable time batting away inconsequential and irrelevant suggestions. And this was one case where time was already their enemy. He felt they were coming in way behind the action, and he needed to get the investigation up and running quickly.

Spence led the meeting and stood at the incident board with pen in hand,

"This is where her body was found." Identifying a stretch of track carrying the London-bound trains. Placed beside it, was a close-up of the victim, the image of a pathetic little body lying face down in the mud.

"Now, considering that this stretch of track was closed for the weekend because maintenance and repairs were taking place further down the line. Then, our time period is between eleven-thirty pm on Friday the seventh of December, when the last train came through, and three pm on Sunday the ninth of December, when the subsequent train came through. We are assuming of course, that if she was there before the last train, then someone would have seen her."

He paused momentarily to check his notes,

"Lividity evidence proves she was on her back when she died, which is not how we found her. She was also out of rigor. So, firstly, she was kept somewhere for about twenty-four hours before being moved. Secondly, it would be unlikely anyone would try to dispose of a body in daylight, wouldn't it? I would therefore suggest we focus on the hours between sunset and sunrise as when she would be most likely to have been taken trackside. Harris, check on those times please, and inform everyone else."

"Yes sir." A subdued smile signified his pleasure at being back on the team.

"And, when we're able to confirm how they got onto the tracks, we can then check any CCTV available, and carry out door to door in those areas. Someone must have seen something."

Spence looked around the room,

"Any comments?"

DS Sarah Bloom raised her hand. In fact, she was always the first to start the ball rolling, and Spence was banking on it. She is seen as the backbone of the department, supportive to a fault, intuitive and tough. She is approachable, and resourceful and encourages discussion, which is not always welcomed by the DCI, but seen by Spence as necessary to keep his finger on the button. If there's an issue among the officers or a gripe about working practices, he wants to know about it. He wants it to be aired, and not fester under the premise that all is well.

"Yes, Sarah."

"Why was she left there at all? Surely, there are better places to dispose of a body. Places where they haven't got to take any risks. I mean, the tracks are visible not only to the rear of some properties but there are two or more blocks of flats that overlook them."

DC Chris Sparkes, a new member of the team, transferred over from the fraud squad, spoke up,

"If they left her when it was dark, I doubt residents in the flats would be looking out the window. I think their intention was to make it look like suicide. To lay her on the track expecting a train to run over her."

"Why wasn't she on the track then?" asked Harris.

"Perhaps they knew the line would be closed, but got spooked by something, possibly railwaymen approaching, panicked and didn't finish the job."

"I think that makes sense," said Spence, "that they didn't want her to be recognised, but why? And who the hell is she?"

"I'm going to visit all local schools today to see if anyone can identify her," said DC Peter Hearn. Another new member, and ex-military police. "And I've also put calls into Social Services, but I haven't had any response from them yet."

Spence gave a frustrated sigh, "Keep at it. Go to their offices if you have to. We need to know if she is, or has ever been in care, and let me know if you get any luck at the schools."

DC Sophie Steele then raised her hand. She's recently qualified and is considered by DCI Fielding to be the one to watch. Although petite and benefitting from a butter wouldn't melt demeanour, her fervour for the role, and the zeal with which she discharges her duties, is drawing the attention of her superiors. Needless to say, with her abundance of enthusiasm, this star in the making is finding it difficult to win over her colleagues.

"I read that she had recently had her nails manicured. Why not visit all the local nail parlours and ask if they can shed any light on who she may be? There can't be too many girls her age having French manicures. She should be memorable."

"I like that Sophie, good idea. Sarah, can you do that please, and take Harris with you. And Sophie, check in the yellow pages as I know many nail beauticians work from home. They will need to be contacted and appointments made for officers to visit them."

Harris was disappointed that he was picked to accompany DS Bloom. He was hoping for a job where he could use his advanced research skills. Plus, at this moment in time, he didn't particularly want to do face-to-face, and he also didn't want another female officer as his oppo. But in fairness, it's highly unlikely that he and Sarah would get involved and make life complicated for him again. She was his senior in both years and rank, is happily married to another sergeant and is the mother of two girls. She is also known to be understanding and will undoubtedly carry him if he starts to wobble. Which is probably why Spence chose her.

"I want someone in the parks too. Speak to the wardens, you never know, one of them might have seen her about," suggested Spence.

"I can do that after I've finished checking with the schools," blurted Hearn.

"I can help too after I've checked the remaining CCTV footage sent in," said Sparkes.

"Is this from the front or rear of the properties?

"The rear sir."

"And nothing so far of any use then Chris?"

"No. There are only a few commercial properties with cameras at the rear, and so far, they haven't caught any unusual activity."

"What about the CCTV on the road or CCTV from the railway station?"

"Much the same I'm afraid – nothing unusual, and it hasn't helped that two of their cameras were out of order."

"Bloody hell! We're not getting a break, are we?" Frustrated, he began to pace up and down before settling on his favourite position, straddling the desk,

"So, we still need to identify how they got trackside. Let's think this through again. What are the options?"

Harris raised his hand, "On Google Earth, I identified several places it might be possible to access the track, one in particular, just before the bridge as the line branches off."

"Great. Print them all off for me Harris, and we can send some officers out to see if any are viable."

Spence scanned the room, but it seemed nobody had anything else to offer.

"Well, if there are no more suggestions, I can tell you that forensics are examining our young victim's clothing for any DNA or trace evidence, but it did rain heavily, so I'm not holding out too much hope on that one. But I think that's all we can do until we find out who she is. Good luck everybody, I know it's going to be a challenge with so little to go on, but we need some progress today, otherwise, we have to go to the media for help in identifying her, and that all takes time, so we really want to try and avoid that if we can."

14:00

DC Peter Hearn had spent a good part of the day trawling around the schools, speaking with office staff, and looking at yearbooks, but hadn't identified the victim as one of their students. He had now positioned himself at the main gate of the community park. He'd been told that it was a popular hangout for the secondary school kids and had arranged to meet with one of the wardens.

It was probably only five minutes or so that Hearn had to wait, but he was cold and disappointed with the lack of reward for all his efforts. Into the mix, if you add his difficulties adjusting to life outside the army, then you produce this morose individual with a sour face, who was stamping up and down, broadcasting his annoyance at being kept waiting.

In the military police, he was used to giving orders, to throwing his weight about, of which he had plenty to throw. Standing at six feet, four inches, with the muscular symmetry of a bodybuilder, he was both an impressive specimen of a man and an intimidating one. He had the power, the status, and the respect from all ranks. He was an enforcer and carried out his duties to the nth degree. But now, it was as if he'd fallen from grace. He felt like a foot soldier, and it didn't sit well with him. His plan was to rise through the ranks as quickly as possible, and with this case, he now had an opportunity to catch the eye of the ones that matter in his quest for advancement. He knew Spence wanted progress, therefore Hearn needed to impress Spence. For that, he had to return to the station with a good lead, and his last chance to get one was with the warden, who was now limping towards him.

He was a tall, thin man, wearing a municipal, heavy brown donkey jacket, a black knitted balaclava, and a grey stripe scarf hung about his neck. On his hands, he wore enormous suede mittens, and in one he held a clutch of jangling keys. It was immediately evident that the warden had a stammer, and first impressions suggested he also had an intellectual disability. Inevitably, his stammer delayed and prolonged what he planned to say, but never-the-less, he wasn't reluctant to speak and seemed keen to help.

He told Hearn that he'd had an occasion recently to eject a group of teenagers from the park because he caught them smoking - he suspected it was weed. He thought he had seen a girl who resembled the description, and that it could have been the girl in the group. He said there was one male in particular who was very aggressive, spiteful, and nasty. He was much taller and older than the rest, perhaps sixteen or seventeen, and in his words was 'full of crap'. This comment Hearn attributed to the fact that the warden has an obvious physical disability, a pronounced speech impediment, and an overabundance of spital that collected at the side of his mouth. No doubt this individual saw the warden as fodder for their entertainment and subjected him to taunts and humiliation. The other members of the group, of which there were two more boys and this one girl, the warden thought was younger, most likely about fourteen.

Hearn was desperate to know if it was the same girl and made an ill-judged decision to stray from best police practice and produced the original forensic photo for the warden to look at.

Not surprisingly, he reeled back at the sight of it,

"Oh! She's dead isn't she!" he spluttered.

"Yes, she is I'm afraid. Do you recognise her?"

The warden didn't reply immediately. He kept his head down, staring intently at the image.

"Is this the girl they found by the track?"

"Yes." replied Hearn abruptly. And repeated, "Do you recognise her?"

"I do. It's her - it's the girl in the group."

Hearn's delighted reaction to the warden's positive ID could have been both inappropriate and uncomfortable if the warden had seen it. But fortunately, he was still engaged with the photo.

Now in official detective mode, Hearn asked,

"Can you remember what day and time you saw them?"

The warden was slow to reply. "Yes, I think so."

His hesitancy was most likely because he had to recall two pieces of information, but Hearn was eager for answers. He didn't stop to think about the difficulties the warden may have in remembering and believed his indecision to be a reluctance to answer. He was losing patience fast and in a raised voice asked firmly,

"And when was that?"

The warden clearly felt intimidated and stepped back trying to distance himself from him. But Hearn continued to invade his personal space, staring him down, and pressing him for an answer,

"It's not a difficult question matey, when was it?"

The warden was confused. He knew when it was, but was struggling to remember the date,

"It was my first day back off leave."

Hearn let out a sigh of frustration, "And when was that?" he snapped.

The warden thought about it – it wasn't easy for him. You could tell by his troubled expression that he was trying hard to remember,

"I think that would have been last Wednesday."

"Okay, so that would have been the fifth and approximately what time was it?" With not a please or thank you and keeping his head down while writing in his notebook, meant he had no finger on the pulse of their interaction either.

The warden seemed unsure but thought it was probably a quarter, or perhaps, a half hour after his afternoon break, and he had that at around two, to two-thirty. But then he wasn't sure,

"Perhaps it was earlier – it sometimes is if I'm cold. I can't get too cold with my conditions you see."

Showing a total indifference to the warden's ailments or his well-being, Hearn continued to probe, "What was she wearing?"

The warden understood the question, but thinking was becoming stressful. He tapped the side of his head for help,

"Blue Jeans, I think. But I'm not sure, they could have been black, and a white, no, maybe pink top."

Hearn gasped, "But she was definitely wearing jeans. Yes?"

No reply was forthcoming from the warden, only a vacant expression that showed he'd had enough. But Hearn, if he did notice the plight of this poor man, chose to ignore it, and launched into a further barrage of questions.

"What about the boys? What did they look like? What were they wearing? Could you identify them if you saw them again?"

Surprisingly, the warden responded, but it lacked both confidence and conviction,

"Yes, I think so. I might be able to. But I'm getting confused now."

"Have a good think matey. Is there anything? Anything else you can remember?"

"No," the warden answered bluntly. "And I might be a little slow officer, but I'm not simple, or stupid. I would help if I could."

For Hearn, the penny had dropped. He wasn't the enforcer in the army anymore, and he'd handled this chap all wrongly. It was obvious at the outset that the warden was a special soul, and to get the most out of him needed a far gentler approach. One that recognised his needs and gave him time to think and respond, and now, Hearn was feeling regretful. At that point, his mobile began to ring.

It was the secretary at the high school. She'd decided to check the records from previous years and had identified a girl, whom she considered would be fifteen by now, and who never attended. The case had been referred to Social Services. Her name was Gemma Willis, and the address given at the time was twenty Edwin Street. Hearn called Spence at once, who in turn called Sarah, and they all arranged to meet. Hearn took the warden's name, address, and phone number, thanked him, and said he would be in touch to arrange a time when he could speak with him again. The warden, who had now decided that he really didn't like Hearn at all, gave no reply, opting instead for a look of contempt.

15:45

DS Sarah Bloom had grown up in the area and knew Edwin Street well. It ran parallel to the highway and was always considered to be an insignificant and quiet thoroughfare. But as with all things, development and progress create change, and it's now a rat run for those inconsiderates who want to avoid the three sets of lights on the main drag. The majority of dwellings are terraced council properties, and the majority of residents are those rehoused following the destruction order of the nearby post-war housing estate, some five years earlier.

On arrival, she observed vehicles were standing bonnet to bumper on both sides of the street, and knowing it was going to be near impossible for them to park, called and suggested that they all meet at the pub just around the corner. Spence agreed. He said that he knew the landlord, and it wouldn't be a problem. Hearn arrived shortly after, followed almost immediately by Spence, who was surprised to see Sarah on her own. She explained that she'd dropped Harris off for his compulsory, psyche evaluation. He hated it, but it was a necessary evil in order for him to return to work.

Sarah and Hearn got into Spence's car and began feeding back on their day. Hearn reported on his conversation with the warden, albeit abridged, and said that he'd positively identified the girl as being with the group of youths in the park on the fifth of December. Spence was keen to hear more from the warden and instructed Hearn to get him in for further questioning.

Sarah reported that three out of the nine nail parlours they visited, had seen a client in the past two weeks, who wasn't one of their regulars, and who had wanted a French manicure. But none were able to recognise her from their description. However, they learned that the technicians take images of their work and upload them onto social media. On examining the uploads for the time period, Harris had decided that they should all be compared with the victim's nails. But one, in particular, appeared to be the hand of a much younger female, he also noticed a crescent-shaped scar at the base of the thumb, on the right hand. It was taken at 'Nailicious' on Wednesday, the twenty-eighth of November, at three-thirty pm, and he was going to ask the pathologist if the victim had the same scar. However, the girl's name in the diary was Sienna, and not Gemma. But a further reason to continue investigating, was that the phone number she gave, was now unobtainable.

As they turned into the street, the light of day had given way to the inevitable darkness. Hearn identified that number twenty would be on the left at the far end of the road.

Spence didn't mind the walk; it would give him time to think. He was hoping that whoever answered the door would declare that Gemma was safe and well, and in her room. But he had a gut feeling that it might not be the case and was mentally preparing himself for the heart-wrenching notification of death to her parents.

A couple of heavy knocks on the weathered door had alerted an occupant, who could now be heard moving slowly along the passage towards them. It was only a small, terraced house, it wouldn't have had a long passageway, but it appeared to be taking the individual much longer than expected to reach the door. Spence predictably, and understandably became suspicious. He wasn't sure of what, but had decided it was very odd behaviour, and the expression on the faces of both Bloom and Hearn confirmed the same bafflement. He knocked again.

"Can you come to the door, please? It's the police."

With that, came a rush of activity in the passage. Spence tried looking through the letter box to see what was going on, but it had one of those brush, draft excluders hanging behind the opening that obscured his view.

"Be there in just a moment," called a woman from inside.

It wasn't a moment at all. It was more like a couple of minutes, but there was nothing the trio could do, but wait. Eventually, the door began to open, and standing before them was a middle-aged woman with shoulder-length blonde hair, wearing a rabbit-in-the-headlights expression that confirmed, she'd definitely been up to something in those few minutes.

"Are you Mrs Willis?" asked Spence.

Moving out over the threshold, and pulling the door behind her, she replied in a soft voice,

"I am officer." Before falling victim to a sudden, sharp, smoker's hack.

Spence was sure that the pungent, slightly floral smell about her, was cannabis, and believed it was being smoked in the house. Which would explain why she was so reluctant to open the door, she was probably finding somewhere to hide her stash. But today, he would have to overlook it, that was until he knew whether or not their victim was her daughter.

"Mrs Willis, is Gemma at home?"

She started to bite her lip, "No. She isn't. Why?"

Spence needed more information from her before divulging why.

"When was the last time you saw her?"

Looking up momentarily for inspiration, she seemed to suddenly remember,

"It was on Thursday morning."

At this point, to her surprise, the door was pulled away from her grasp, and a small, slightly built man, wearing dirty low-slung jeans and a grubby white T-shirt, moved out onto the step beside her.

"What's going on Jude?" he demanded. Then, addressed Spence directly. "And who are you?"

"My name is Detective Inspector Jack Spence, and I would like to speak with Gemma please."

"Well, you can't. She's not here." spurted Mrs Willis. The pair began to back up inside the house. Obviously, for them, the conversation was over.

"Hang on. Indulge me please Mrs Willis, just so we know we're speaking about the same child. How old is your daughter Gemma?"

Mrs Willis, who had now pushed past the man, and moved fully into the passage, called out,

"She's fourteen. Why? What d'you want with her?"

This was not what Spence wanted to hear at all. His train of thought now was not on breaking his sensitive news, but on treating the pair as hostile, and possible suspects in the girl's murder.

Spence put a hand on the door, preventing the man from closing it,

"I need to come in and talk to you. Now!"

The man held firm against the door. Then, when realising Spence wasn't backing down, and they were not going to go away, relented and ushered them in.

As Spence entered, he turned to the man and asked, "And who are you, sir?"

"I'm Reg Willis. Gemma's old man."

One by one, they filed along the short passageway, and into the living room. Mrs Willis sat on the grey corduroy sofa, and Reg Willis sat beside her. Spence chose the armchair facing the couple, who were now in a huddle, holding hands and looking worried. Bloom and Hearn remained standing.

Spence introduced themselves, and Mrs Willis, in turn, reiterated that her name was Jude.

"Did you report Gemma as missing?"

The pair glanced at each other with a look that suggested Spence was speaking in a foreign language and gave no reply.

He asked again, "Did you report your fourteen-year-old daughter as missing?"

Reg was shuffling, and appeared to be uncomfortable, "We didn't know she was missing."

"You didn't know?" asked Spence in disbelief. "Your wife told me she hadn't seen her since Thursday morning, and it's now Tuesday! Mrs Willis, Jude, where did you think she was?"

Reg put an arm around his wife's shoulders, and answered for her,

"Where she's been for the last six weeks, in Darcy House."

Spence looked over to Hearn, "That's the home for adolescents, isn't it? Didn't you contact them?"

"Yes, I did and I'm still waiting for a response, sir."

Spence, the consummate professional, made no remark, but his prolonged glare sent a clear message to Hearn - he was in trouble. Spence distinctly remembered telling him to go to the Social Services offices if they hadn't come back to him. If he had done as ordered, they would not have been chasing their tails all day.

Spence turned to Reg, "How long has she been in care?"

"Since late October," he replied, with a sadness in his voice belonging to the bereaved.

Spence, in tune with the couple's pain, asked respectfully,

"And why was she in care?"

Jude burrowed her head into her husband's neck and sobbed into a tissue. Reg put an arm around her, caressed her hair and kissed her head tenderly. A moment of silence followed, as he too struggled to bring his emotions under control before being able to speak. He told them, that Gemma had been a problem child for a number of years. That she would not go to school, locked herself in her room, and point blank refused to cooperate with anyone who offered to help.

"She was my daughter, but I had no control over her!" he shouted. Fighting back the tears. "She wouldn't do as she was told or listen to anyone. Not me or her mum, not her family, not her doctor. No-one. We were at our wits end with her behaviour. But then it took a turn for the worse when, just after Easter, we noticed that she'd stopped eating, and worse still when we also found out she was self-harming. We tried everything, but nothing worked. She was getting thinner, and weaker. So, Social Services said they would arrange for her to be looked after for a while. They said they thought she had a mental illness and needed professional help."

Reading into what Reg had said, Spence suspected, that it would have been more a case, that Social Services decided the parents were unable to cope any longer. But he wasn't going to condemn them for that. They'd obviously suffered years of stress caring for their daughter and helping someone overcome issues with their mental health is a difficult job, he knew that from his first-hand experience with Harris. By their reactions, he was sure they would have tried their best. He was also sure that their daughter Gemma was the victim. He now needed confirmation.

"Do you have a photo of Gemma please?"

Reg went over to the bureau, opened the drawer, and handed Spence a photo of his daughter taken at a family gathering. She was a year or two younger, fresh-faced, and well-covered, not like the little waif on the track, but it was definitely her. He now had to deliver the worst news a parent could hear.

THREE

Tuesday 11th December – 07:30

DCI Dave Fielding sat relaxed in his executive chair taking notes, as he listened intently to Spence feeding back on the progress of the investigation so far. He would, in turn, be reporting the progress to his superior, DSU Merriman, and although Fielding was the darling of the station, he wouldn't be afforded any slack.

"Yesterday, officers visited several sites where the offenders could, without too much difficulty, have accessed the track, and for the identification of these, we can thank Harris," Spence stated proudly. Seizing the opportunity to sing Harris' praises in an effort to reassure Fielding that he didn't need to worry about the lad. But Fielding saw right through it,

"Go on," he snapped. And waved him on to continue, with a look that implied he should have known better.

Spence gave a little smile, and pointing to a location on his map said,

"We are focusing our efforts on this site in particular."

"And why is that significant?"

"Because a resident who lives close to the site, her house being the last in a terrace of six and adjacent to the narrow unadopted slip road, said that she'd seen a black van parked up at about eight-thirty on Saturday the eighth, and that two rail workers had got out with what she thought was a large tool bag, and walked towards the track. She then went to make a phone call, and when she returned to the kitchen about fifteen minutes later, she saw that the van had left.

"What made her think they were rail workers?"

Spence checked his notes, "She said that they were both wearing dark jackets that had a Hi-Vis panel across the back."

"But lots of men wear those. Surely, there must have been something else."

"No, apparently not. I think, because rail workers were often seen in the slip road, and because they were walking casually towards the track, she assumed that's what they were. I expect it would only have raised her suspicion if she'd seen them running towards it."

"That tells me that these two men knew both the area and that it was used by rail workers. It doesn't tell me that these two men are in any way connected to the crime, but if the time frame fits and we get further evidence to confirm them as suspects, then, considering their audacity, we're looking for a couple of nasty, dangerous bastards who are used to that sort of work."

"Absolutely."

"What are we doing to find the van?"

Spence let out a sigh, "There's very little we can do. She didn't know the make, only that it was large, like a transit. Sophie is over there now going through pictures of vans with her, to see if she can recognise it. We're also checking to see if a black van has been reported as significant in any other cases and, of course, we're hoping we get some CCTV."

"And what about the investigation at Darcy House?"

"I spoke with the staff, and they were all under the impression that Gemma had gone home for a long weekend. The duty manager said she left in a cab on Thursday at twelve-thirty after lunch. The problem is, we've spoken to all the cab firms in the area, and none had a pick-up from Darcy at that time."

"It seems like it wasn't a cab at all then?"

"No. It seems increasingly unlikely that it was. However, two members of staff agree it was a white Mercedes, and thought it had decals on the side of it but couldn't remember what it was."

Fielding stopped writing and tapped his pen on the table, "Someone is lying then."

"It seems that way, doesn't it? We are checking with all the firms' clients who hired a cab at that time to confirm that they exist, and that the job actually took place. But I think it's more likely that if it was a cab, and he was working off the radar, that he wouldn't have recorded it in his driver's log."

"Was there no number plate caught on CCTV?"

"No. Apparently, it conveniently went offline."

"Okay, that's too much of a coincidence. So coming at it another way. Surely, whoever organised the home visit would have arranged the cab and been in contact with the family."

"Yes, I agree but the family were not expecting her home, and the manager who was on duty at the time, a chappie called Freddie Turner, cannot be traced at the moment. I've got men outside his flat waiting for him to return."

"Did you have any luck speaking to the other six residents?"

"We hit a wall of silence there, which I expected we would. There are three girls on the second floor, Gemma would have been the fourth, and three boys on the third floor. All were very upset by the news, but the police are not well-liked by these youngsters. Their interaction with us, has in the main, been negative. So, to get anywhere with them, we need to speak to them individually, and with someone, they trust at their side."

"And do you have someone in mind?"

"Yes. The one person the kids were asking for, especially the girls, was their social worker, Sammi Mancini, so I'm meeting with her at Darcy this morning to enlist her help. I couldn't speak to her yesterday as she was travelling back from a conference in Scotland. Bloom and Harris will also be in attendance, carrying out an in-depth search of Gemma's room, if there's something to be found, those two will find it."

Fielding nodded his approval, then leaned forward, looked Spence straight in the eye, and asked,

"Now tell me about Hearn. And I don't want any Spence whitewash."

Spence reluctantly admitted that he was disappointed with Hearn's performance the day before and told Fielding the reason, that Hearn hadn't visited Social Services as asked to do so in the briefing.

"So, in essence, a whole bloody day wasted because 'Rambo' Hearn didn't do as ordered?"

Spence grimaced, "He certainly didn't prioritise his work well enough, but I don't get the impression he's incompetent."

"Jack! He's not exactly new to the job is he!"

"He is really." argued Spence, "he wasn't ever a detective, he's learning on the job like the others."

"He sounds like a liability to me! If you don't want him on the team, just say so, and I'll transfer him to a desk job somewhere."

Spence, who was always very protective of his team, even the lame ducks, which he felt the need to nurture and develop, baulked against the idea of moving Hearn on.

"Give him time. He screwed up! I'll sort the lad out."

"Don't spend too much time on it Jack. I need results. Any more screwups and he's out."

Spence didn't like it when Fielding was so unyielding, but as the SIO, he also knew that he'd be under a lot of pressure from DSU Merriman and DCS Black, to clear this case quickly.

It was the time of year when statistics were being compiled, graphs were being drawn and decisions were being made on performance. Detective Chief Superintendent Black wanted to keep his department in the top ten of the Met, and for that, top-down pressure was being applied. CID had the same status as a celebrity. In the public eye, it was both dangerous and glamorous, it was the good defeating the bad, but most importantly, it was essential copy for the tabloids, the public couldn't get enough of it, and therefore, it had to shine.

Harris was waiting outside Spence's office when he returned,

"Sir, I've received an image of the victim's hands from the pathologist, and she has the same scar as that on the hand photographed in the nail parlour."

"Great work lad. That means we need to pay the parlour another visit, don't we? Someone wasn't being truthful."

"Yes sir. Okay to go alone or shall I wait for Sarah?"

"No, I'll send Sparkes to the parlour. I want you to join Sarah at Darcy House. I want a thorough search of Gemma's room and any other room that she used. I will also be there at some point. Let me know if you find anything, and I will call a team meeting for this afternoon so you can add your findings to the victimology. That's all." he said sharply. "And, on your way out ask Hearn to come in please."

Spence was intending to speak to Hearn about his cock-up the day before, to give him a dressing down, and hopefully move forward. But, whilst he was waiting, he read a report that had been left on his desk. It was concerning the hit-and-run of a man the evening before. Witnesses say that it wasn't an accident, it was a deliberate act. They saw a black van leave the road, mount the pavement, mow him down and drive off. The victim hadn't survived, and the case was therefore referred to CID. The victim's name was James Wilson. The name rang a bell, he'd heard or read that name recently. Then he remembered, it was the same name as the park warden. But was it the same man? And was it the same bloody van?

Hearn had now arrived with his report from his interview with the warden in his hand,

"This is my report from yesterday sir." Placing it on the desk.

Spence looked up at him, and then back at his report. He had a bad feeling about this and was almost afraid to open it.

"Did you write it out word for word Hearn?"

"Yes sir. It's all there."

Spence opened the folder and started reading. It wasn't a long report because their interaction had been brief, but Spence seemed to dwell on it. He kept returning to the exchange where the warden asked if it was the girl on the tracks.

"Dear God, Hearn! How did he know it was a girl on the tracks? At that point, all anyone knew was that a body had been found!"

Hearn looked ashen. He hadn't picked up on it.

"This man!" shouted Spence. "Is now the victim of a hit-and-run. He's dead! And none of this smells right, does it?"

"It could just be a coincidence sir." came Hearn's pathetic reply.

Spence held his head in his hands, "Strewth man. You are sailing so fucking close to the wind! You need to buck your bloody ideas up!"

Hearn remained silent. He wasn't used to being sworn at, it was usually the other way around. Anyway, what could he say? He knew Spence was right. He wasn't on the ball and deeply regretted his handling of the warden.

"Now!" roared Spence. Shoving the case file across the desk. "Your first job is to ID this man. Is he the same James Wilson you met in the park? Secondly, I want to be the first to know if it is! I don't want to learn anything tomorrow, that I should have learned today! Got it!"

"Yes sir!" he replied. Standing to attention.

Spence wasn't impressed. He didn't want subservience, just someone who used their brain would be nice.

"I'm off to the morgue now to meet the parents for the formal identification, and then I'm visiting Darcy House to interview Gemma's social worker. If there's anything you think I should know, call me immediately." And with that, he swigged down the remains of his cold tea, grabbed his keys off the desk and made for the door. Hearn let out a sigh of relief as it closed behind him.

Darcy House – 09:00

Except for the sign at the side of the entrance door, Darcy House was inconspicuous as a residential care home for adolescents. The facade of multiple windows, set in a standard geometric design, blended in perfectly with every other block of flats along the street. Yet the rooms behind these windows were not parts of a greater residence, they didn't contribute to the needs and requirements of a family. Instead, they each housed one lonely, troubled, and troublesome soul, who for some, would remain a guest within those walls for a significant period of time. But for the majority, it functioned as a revolving door in the care system. Care being the operative word. And the reasons why kids found themselves in a taxi bound for Darcy are extensive, but so too, is the list of failures it spewed out and into the prison system.

As with most institutions, there was a regime. A daily timetable intended to offer a balanced programme of therapy, education and personal development sessions that focused on fostering good social and life skills. However, such a timetable requires specialists and support staff to deliver the content. It requires organisation and resources to support the specialists, and of course, it requires a substantial amount of funding to make it all work.

In reality, the funding received was a quarter of what was needed to provide such a programme. This meant that the salaries they could offer fell way below what a specialist would command, and subsequently attracted a lesser qualified, lesser experienced staff member. Furthermore, with the inevitable reduction in support staff, the full and varied timetable was also reduced to a bare minimum. The biggest casualty of the cuts being the personal development sessions, now replaced by 'personal opportunities for reflection'. In other words, the kids were consigned to their rooms for several hours a day, to dwell on their unhappy lives, and think dark thoughts. Is it any wonder then, that the programme's success was stunted?

Sarah Bloom had driven to Darcy straight from dropping off her kids at school. She was sitting in the reception area next to the Christmas tree, waiting for Harris to arrive. She could see John Taylor, the duty manager, moving about in his office. He appeared to be very busy indeed, shuffling papers, then moving them from one side of the room to the other, and each time, he would look over in her direction. And you don't have to be a detective to recognise when someone is unnerved by your presence, but why?

Harris had now arrived and was eager to get started. This was his sort of job, surveying, sifting, rummaging, ferreting, and employing his extraordinary talent for discovering the previously undetected. Sarah complimented his set of skills with her own extraordinary talent for intuitiveness, that sixth sense of hers being instrumental in the downfall of many a villain. So today, these two super-beings would need to do their stuff and find something that could lead the team to understand why Gemma was murdered.

Gemma's room was on the second floor opposite the stairwell. Her neighbour on the left was Jasmine, a fourteen-year-old who had been a resident for the last ten months following removal from her family home. And it wasn't the first time either that her mother's heroin addiction had bought her a ticket to Darcy. This morning she had declined to have breakfast and was sitting, crossed-legged on her bed, scrolling through her phone. She glanced up as the pair approached Gemma's door.

"She didn't like it when people went through her things," she said mournfully.

Sarah leant against the doorframe and smiled at her,

"I'm sure she didn't. I wouldn't like it either."

Then in a raised, emotional voice, she asked, "Why do it then?"

Sarah thought for a moment before answering. Jasmine was angered by their presence. She didn't want them in the home and was wanting to protect her friend's privacy. Why?

"Jasmine. We need to find out what happened to Gemma and looking in her room will help us to do that."

"I don't see how! She didn't have nothing!"

And that remark, coupled with Jasmine's attitude, told Sarah that Gemma did indeed have something, and that Jasmine knew what it was. She was itching to continue with the questioning, but protocol had to be followed. Permission would have to be sought first and an appropriate adult present. For now, she had no choice but to focus on the search and organise to speak to Jasmine later.

Harris had made entry to the room and was systematically removing items from the top drawer of a chest of six,

"She didn't have many clothes, and what she did have were cheap and cheerful I think." Holding up a T-shirt for Sarah to examine and confirm.

Sarah felt the fabric and looked for a maker's label, "Oh yeah. That's a really cheap garment, off the market I expect."

Harris continued his search of the other drawers, while Sarah's attention was on examining the dressing table.

"Sarah! I'm not an expert, but isn't this a designer label?"

He'd found a pale blue, silky, pull-on top and the label read 'Dior'.

Sarah wasn't convinced. "I think that's probably off the market too."

"What? A knockoff?" He thought it looked like the real thing.

Sarah drew his attention to the label, "A knockoff Harris, is a copy of a piece of designer clothing, it doesn't have the brand label in it. This poorly made brand label tells me it's an out-and-out fake, but it could still have been bought on the market. We need to pay them a visit. It looks fairly new, doesn't it, so perhaps they may remember her and when she bought it."

Beside the drawers was a green plush tub chair, and alongside that, a washbasin.

"That's an odd place to have a chair, isn't it?" remarked Sarah, "especially one like that, it would get splashed and ruin the fabric, wouldn't it? But look Harris, it doesn't appear to have a mark on it."

"It hasn't been there long enough to get splashed then, has it?"

"No. It's been put there recently, but why?

"The one thing that stands out, is that it doesn't have legs. The chair sits firmly on the floor.

Let's look underneath."

Sarah lifted the chair out into the room. There was nothing stuck to the base, and nothing immediately stood out as suspicious. Harris squatted down and began to feel over the grey carpet tiles.

"What do we have here?" Identifying a tile in the middle of a set of three. "It's covering up a hole of some kind."

Sarah also felt the tiles, "I think so too."

Carefully, Harris removed the tile. At one end, up against the wall was a hole for the water pipes to pass down to the floor below, and in front, where the two planks didn't quite meet, was a small gap, and placed inside was a tablet of some kind.

"I think that's an iPad," said Harris.

Sarah nodded in agreement, "I'll call in forensics and let Spence know what we've found."

FOUR

Tuesday 11th December – 14:00

Originally the briefing was scheduled for 13:00, but Hearn's bombshell that the victim of the hit-and-run, James Wilson, was indeed the park warden, had caused all manner of problems. Spence was immediately engaged in awkward discussions to have the case transferred to his team, Fielding was being hassled by Merriman for an explanation as to why Spence was on the back foot, and Merriman was in turn, being hassled by the DCS and the press, who had now discovered a connection between Gemma and the warden.

It appears that a journalist had in the course of his enquiries, uncovered that the warden did odd jobs for Darcy House, and had done so for the past year. What's more, he also discovered that the unfortunate warden had found it necessary to make a complaint because some of the residents had mentally abused him. Fielding was furious that CID was seen as wanting in the detection department and aimed his wrath squarely at Hearn. That was until Spence intervened and said that nobody would have thought to ask questions at Darcy about the warden.

For CID, this information had put the investigation into the realms of a double murder and a conspiracy. The black van was now highly significant, and the hunt intensified for the two men seen at the tracks. Spence, however, was in his element juggling all these balls, it was where his talents lie. But it's hard to juggle with so many people on your back, and he was feeling the pressure.

Spence and Fielding stood at the whiteboard, while DSU

Merriman, who had not been expected, and whose presence had changed the atmosphere from focused but relaxed, to focused and intense, had propped himself up against the wall just inside the entrance. A favoured position of his, as from here he was able to observe all parts of the room.

Spence opened the briefing,

"First, I would like to thank everybody for their effort to date, and for giving their time to this investigation."

At which point, Fielding's prolonged glare in the direction of Hearn, was widely observed by the others. Hearn kept his head down. Spence continued,

"Following a search carried out by Sarah and Harris, where an iPad was discovered in our victim's room, Darcy House is now the focus of our enquiries. I can confirm that the iPad belonged to Gemma, and on examination, I can tell you that what we discovered is very disturbing." Shaking his head in disgust at what he knew and was soon to share.

"Her browsing history includes many visits to chatrooms where suicide is discussed, and in my opinion, even encourages it. This was one very lonely, and very unhappy girl, which is probably why it was so easy for someone, whom she refers to as the shepherd, to befriend her. Further investigations are being carried out to obtain a full history of her interaction with this individual. However, I can confirm, from the many photos in the gallery, that she had been coerced into exposing herself to him, and into performing degrading sexual acts for his gratification. And predictably, she was unable to stop her participation."

Spence then waved a sheet of paper in the air.

"This is just one of many exchanges with the shepherd. It is dated just over two weeks ago. She had begged him to allow her to stop, and this is his reply.

'Sweetheart, you know that's not going to happen. You are mine for as long as I want you. If you tell, my sweetheart, you know what will happen.'

And this I believe refers to an earlier threat, where he tells her that he has her on video and will upload it onto the internet if she tries to leave him.

The room went deathly quiet. Each officer, alone with their thoughts, absorbing the information.

"Our tech boys are working hard to identify who this man is, but they fear, due to the fact that anonymity reigns supreme in these chatrooms, and coupled with the lack of stewardship, that the chance of finding him through this route is unlikely. Therefore, it's up to us to hunt for the shepherd.

We need to leave no stone unturned in our effort to identify him, track him down, and lock him up before any other children are abused, or worse, killed. It may be that we have to resort to using an undercover officer posing as a child to unmask him."

And as he drew breath, in that split second, every officer had raised their arm to offer their service as the imposter. Spence was not surprised; he had an amazing team and would expect nothing less.

"Thank you one and all," he said with pride. And continued,

"From the browsing history, we are able to say with certainty that the online relationship continued while she was a resident at Darcy House, and many of the exchanges confirm that he knew she was in care and has knowledge about drugs."

He paused for a moment, clearly affected by the emotive content of his report.

"It seems the only good thing that happened to this poor little lass as a result of the move, was finding two friends. One is Jasmine Wright, the young girl in the room next to hers, and the other, is with a sixteen-year-old boy called Sean

McKinney." He paused again to gather his thoughts.

"However, we can't rule out the possibility that she had a sexual relationship with this boy, and that he could also be responsible for transmitting the Chlamydia disease. Unfortunately, he is not a resident, and officers are currently engaged in trying to locate him."

Sarah raised her hand,

"Is it possible, because the shepherd appears to have known about Gemma's problems that he is a professional of some kind?"

Spence nodded, "Considering Fentanyl was used. Yes, he could be a medical professional. But he could equally be a criminal involved in the drugs trade. Many street drugs are laced with it. At fifty times more potent than Heroin, and one hundred times more potent than Morphine, it makes the drug cheaper to manufacture. And while we're on the subject of drugs, in the light of information obtained off the iPad confirming their use while Gemma was at Darcy, I have ordered a search of the building."

Spence looked around the room.

"DC Sparkes, what did you find out about the cab?"

Sparkes stood to report on his findings, which caused a few titters. They either do that as a matter of course in his previous squad, or it was the Merriman effect, Sarah suspected the latter.

"I have organised for each cab company that operates a white Mercedes or has freelance drivers who own one, to provide details of the drivers, and background checks are underway."

"Has anybody been identified as a person of interest?" asked Fielding.

"No sir, not yet."

"Okay, thank you. And I've just been informed that Freddie Turner, the House manager on duty the day Gemma left in a cab, has been detained. I will be questioning him shortly and you can sit in."

"Thank you, sir. Do you want feedback on my visit to the nail parlour now?"

"Yep, go on lad," said Spence.

"I spoke with the beautician who manicured Gemma's nails. She said that she didn't recognise her by our description, but identification of the crescent scar had jogged her memory. She said that the appointment was made for her as a gift experience and that a young boy, about sixteen or seventeen, tall with dark hair, was waiting for her when she left. I asked who bought the experience, and she said it was another young girl about fourteen, with long dark hair, and that she paid cash."

"Great. Thanks, Chris. I suspect the boy was Sean McKinney." Then turned to Sarah, "Could the girl be Jasmine?"

"Possibly sir, she does have long dark hair."

"Good, I feel like we're getting somewhere. Follow that up please."

Spence surveyed the room and continued, "I'm sure you have all been briefed as to the direction this investigation is now taking. No longer are we working to identify Gemma's murderers alone, but also the murderers of James Wilson, who may well be one of the same. Our second victim was the park warden previously interviewed by DC Hearn. Now, because he did odd jobs for Darcy House, he may or may not have met Gemma before, she had only been a resident for six weeks after all. But I have a feeling, that he was known to the other members of the group he encountered in the park on Wednesday the fifth of December, and the older boy may well be Sean McKinney. So, Hearn. Wilson wasn't the only park warden. Speak with the others. Did they know of any previous issues with this group? Take a photo of McKinney and see if they can identify the older one as him. I also want you to compile a full background check on James Wilson. Speak to his boss, family, and all known associates, even local shopkeepers."

Then Fielding, deeming it necessary to contribute, added, "And a full and complete profile please."

Hearn nodded that he understood, then replied sheepishly, "Yes sir."

You could cut the atmosphere with a knife. Spence then produced a folder and passed it to Sarah,

"Here is the report on my meeting with Sammy Mancini, Darcy's social worker. In there, you will find a full account of Gemma's short life and information on the other residents. I want you and Harris back at Darcy this afternoon, Miss Mancini is expecting you, she will be acting as the appropriate adult for Jasmine's and the other resident's interviews. John Taylor has also been asked to make himself available for an interview. From your report, both he and Jasmine seem to have something to hide, and press Jasmine on whether or not Gemma had a phone. Her parents confiscated her original mobile in an attempt to bring her into line, I have it in my office, but there's nothing of interest on it. We shall of course be following up on her contacts, but I think she had another one. I suspect the shepherd would have given Gemma a mobile so he could keep in contact with her. I also suspect it was a pay-as-you-go, so she could only accept calls. We need to find it."

Then reaching for a second folder and handing it to Sparkes, "I need you to visit the market and I want Sophie Steele to go with you."

Sparkes seemed startled at the order to be paired with Sophie, he didn't think she was that experienced, and anyway, he preferred to work alone. Spence sensed his surprise and asked,

"When was the last time you bought a top off the market Sparkes?" Causing a ripple of laughter from those assembled.

"I haven't sir."

"Exactly."

Then turning to Sophie, who didn't wait for the question, chirped, "All the time, sir."

Sparkes gave a little chuckle, "Got it."

Spence instructed them to seek out stalls selling fake clothing and to take a photo of the Dior garment with them, as it was new, there might be a chance it was still being sold. Then passing over a more recent photo of Gemma, supplied by her parents, he told them to show it around the market and shops in the hope that someone might recognise her as a customer, and hopefully remember if she was with anybody.

Now, with all items on his list covered, and it seemed that everyone had a job to do, it was time to wrap up the briefing.

"That's all for now folks." Raising his hands in thanks, then added, "And I know the shift has officially ended but we really do need to keep at it." In other words, nobody was going home yet.

Darcy House Interviews – 15:40

On arrival at Darcy House, the rear car park was a hive of police activity. Sniffer dogs had been brought in to help with the search for possible illegal drugs, and one had followed a scent to an extinguished bonfire on a small piece of wasteland behind a row of lock-up garages.

It appears that an eagle-eyed resident had been alerted to the fire and made it his business to put it out. He thought kids had started it. Fortunately for the investigation and unfortunately for the offender, it had been a slow burner, and forensics were now sifting through the ashes and bagging the remnants. The most significant to the enquiry was a mobile phone and a duvet with a cover that carried the Darcy logo. It may or may not have belonged to Gemma, but they had to proceed suspecting they were hers until forensics proved otherwise. And this turn of events had put a completely different slant on how they managed their visit today.

With the possibility that Gemma was killed in Darcy House and kept there for at least twenty-four hours before being moved, Darcy would now be deemed a crime scene. Their interview with the manager was going to be their first priority as he would be the one to identify the bedding. He would also be the one to find alternative accommodation for the remaining six residents and arrange for them to attend interviews at the station. However, it was Miss Mancini who was holding the fort in the office and doing her best to organise everything. John Taylor, the manager, was nowhere to be found.

The Market Investigation – 17:00

By four pm it was almost dark, and the arctic blast that had ambushed and buffeted the country for the past few days had turned the road into an ice rink. The heavy traffic was moving, but very slowly, and the short trip to the market had become a long-winded trek, the fifteen-minute journey taking almost an hour.

They parked up behind the café, and on exiting the car were immediately hit with the aroma of burgers and chips. They'd both missed lunch, and that mouth-watering smell was a cruel reminder that they would probably be missing dinner too.

Chris stood out in the crowd, he was not a shopper, and he looked awkward and uncomfortable,

"I don't get it! People are just walking about looking at things, I can't see any buying going on."

He couldn't understand why anyone would go to another stall if the first one had what you were looking for. And no matter how many times Sophie tried to explain that what you're looking for doesn't exist until you've compared it with what you've seen, he still didn't get it.

It was now ten past five, and the market was filling up with people. Most of them were families who had come along to witness the turning on of the Christmas lights at five-fifteen. Then, right on cue, with the flip of a switch, the entire area burst into twinkling light. The crowd cheered and clapped, and the market came alive!

At one end, outside the Dog and Duck pub, which was heaving and spilling out onto the pavement, was the most magnificent Christmas tree. It stood at least twelve feet high and was brimming with baubles and lights. Positioned in a star shape around it were colourful stalls selling food from around the world. The mixture of aromas, from Asian spices and French cheeses to good old-fashioned hotdogs, was intoxicating.

Occupying the middle of the road was a train of stalls that snaked to the shape of the market towards Santa's grotto, and each was draped in fairy lights, glistening garlands, and metres of tinsel in a myriad of colours. Jolly Christmas songs were sung with gusto by the carol singers, who were meandering along the slippery pavements, collecting for local charities. Elves were darting in and out of the stalls giving out treats to the children and at the main road end, a choir from the local church sang and swayed to the music of the High School band.

It was a wonderful festive spectacle, but as much as they wanted to, they couldn't join in with the celebrations. They had a job to do, and both agreed that they needed to split up in order to cover all the ground or they'd be there till Christmas! Sophie took the right side and Chris, the left.

It wasn't an easy task to push through people who had been queueing patiently at the stalls, it took some convincing, and those who refused to step aside, ultimately responded to the wave of a badge. After twenty minutes, Sophie had been marginally more successful than Chris, who had zero to report. She, at least, had found a stall holder who thought he recognised Gemma and offered to call her if he remembered anything else. They met up again at the Scouts' Christmas stall,

"This is useless. Nobody's seen her and I haven't seen one clothes stall," complained Chris. Burying his hands in his pockets and stamping his feet to keep warm.

Sophie smiled, "Yes, it certainly is. We've just caught it all wrong. All these stallholders want to do is make as much money as possible tonight, it's probably one of the best nights in the year for sales. They're certainly not going to waste any valuable time talking to us, are they? And I don't think it's the sort of market to buy clothes, not tonight anyway. Perhaps we need to visit again during the day?"

They both agreed to stop for a cuppa, sit and regroup, and formulate a plan. Sophie commented that she was 'spitting feathers' which made Chris laugh. He was used to hearing the expression from the old-timers up north and didn't expect to hear it from a Londoner. In fact, since moving down to London, he'd found himself on a steep learning curve, there were a lot of things he hadn't expected; to pay fifteen hundred pounds a month on rent for one.

Being his first time down south having been born and bred in the borders, the giveaway to his heritage being Titian red hair, and a soft, warm Scottish accent, he should have done his homework. At twenty-six and having spent all of his life in a rural location, he was itching to taste the big city experience, and when the opportunity came along to work for the Met, he took it. He told Sophie that he enjoyed keeping busy, but sometimes, especially at weekends, he missed the country walks he took with his dog, and the fun he had with his friends on the Tweed. But most of all he missed the cash he had to himself at the end of the month, not so now, it all goes on living expenses.

Sophie enjoyed listening to his stories of rural life, she found his descriptions of the countryside appealing, and his accent charming, mainly because she was an out-and-out townie. Mind you, hailing from South-East London, her accent was also unique. Her English teacher once commented that it should be classed as a dialect. She found it fascinating that it was considered the usual practice to drop a letter from a word, sometimes several letters, and in some cases even create a new word, and still be understood!

The pair were deep in conversation when a scuffle outside drew their attention to the window. A couple of youths were squaring up before being sent packing by a market porter, and as they all moved off, Chris noticed a face in the crowd that he recognised. It was John Taylor. Sophie recognised him too – his photo was pinned to the whiteboard – and now he was a wanted man! He looked worried, almost fretful. They called Spence who ordered them to follow discretely, to keep him updated, and said he was on his way.

Taylor was moving quickly through the market in the direction of the recreation ground. Sophie, being a diminutive five feet, three inches, kept losing her view of him in the sea of heads, but Chris, a six-footer, kept him firmly in his sights. On a couple of occasions when Sophie seemed to get boxed in, he would grab her hand and retrieve her from the huddle.

Their target had now reached the pub. He stopped outside and looked around before entering. In the bustling crowds, he didn't notice Chris snapping away on his phone, but then he'd never met him before. If he was up to no good, it would be Harris that he'd be looking out for.

They followed quickly behind and watched as he perched

himself on a stool at the far end of the bar. It appeared a drink was waiting for him. His hand shook as he lifted the half-pint glass and some of the contents spilt onto his scarf before it reached his lips. The pair decided to sit and watch for what he did next.

Chris tried to convince Sophie that he would have to order a pint as if they both sat with an orange juice, the publican would know they were officers for sure. Sophie agreed so long as he didn't drink it. At this point, the expression on Chris' face was priceless.

The pub was now experiencing a wave of new customers and the queue to get served was three deep.

"At this rate, I won't need to worry about drinking it, I doubt I'll even get to order it." he whinged.

Sophie, who was well aware that Chris was still holding her hand, had decided not to mention it. She quite liked it. He had a strong grip and it made her feel safe. It's amazing how we rationalise something in order to make it feel acceptable, isn't it? Oh dear – I think she's falling.

She looked around, taking it all in, and as she panned past the door to the beer garden, she noticed two men sitting at a table in the corner. They were both wearing black jackets and the one with his back to them had a Hi-Vis panel across the back. Assessing that the jackets looked identical, and that the other man would most likely have the same panel at the back, Sophie thought that they could be the two men with the black van. She pulled her hand away, grabbed Chris' arm to pull him down to her level and whispered in his ear,

"Look behind you at ten o'clock. I think it's the men we're looking for."

Sparkes needed to take a photo and send it to Spence, but how to do it without drawing attention was the problem? Sophie pointed to the tall, glitzy, tinsel-clad plant pot that stood by the garden door.

"Why not take a photo of me posing by the pot? On a wide lens, you could also get the two men into the picture."

Chris thought it was a brilliant idea, and in practice worked well too. In a matter of minutes he had forwarded his photos. The hope was that the one whose face was clearly visible, had previous and that they could get an ID. Now, with the troops on the way, they needed to watch, wait and be ready to follow if any of the three men should leave.

18:10

Conducting surveillance with the aim being to apprehend the suspects, is a difficult job to organise at the best of times. But tonight, when all roads to the targets are closed off, and the public is everywhere, it becomes a nightmare. It was taking some time to develop a strategy, and it wasn't down to procrastination. Spence was working with very little intelligence. He didn't know if any of the men were armed, and this was preventing any attempt at an extraction from the pub for fear they may endanger the public. It had become a waiting game. Only when the men leave, will they be able to approach and apprehend, and the shout will be made on a split-second decision. Officers blended in with the crowd and waited for instructions.

Chris was relaying developments via text message and Sophie had managed to set up a live stream to Spence on her mobile through Facetime. They were quite a double act with the tech, pretending to take photos of each other and making calls. It appeared that the men in black jackets, having just bought a further two pints of ale, were not going anywhere soon. However, John Taylor was not so comfortable. He looked anxious and was constantly watching the door, as if he was expecting someone, and was making his drink last, only the odd sip every few minutes passed his lips. On one occasion he visited the gents toilet, and Chris followed. Sophie was concerned that if he went a second time, that he would get suspicious if Chris followed him in again. But he reassured her, that he didn't need to follow him again because there was no exit from the pub via the gents. The only exits were the front door, a back door at the end of a short passage which was mainly used for deliveries, or through the beer garden.

It was now seven-fifteen, Chris had spent the last fifteen minutes caressing his glass and was beginning to weaken,

"I'm sure someone will notice if it doesn't appear to go down. I should take a good gulp, so it looks like it's being drunk. We don't want to draw attention to ourselves do we?"

He'd barely stopped speaking when a text came through. It was from Spence and read, no! Chris had momentarily forgotten about the live feed and was now feeling thankful that he hadn't followed through on his thought, to sweet-talk Sophie into going out for dinner. He would never have lived it down, that is if he hadn't got the sack. Sophie tapped the table to draw his attention,

"Taylor's on the move." she mouthed.

Chris turned to see him walk around the bar towards the passageway. Sophie informed Spence that Taylor was leaving the pub by the back door, but he told them not to follow. To stay put and maintain their observation of the two men, and that he would pick up Taylor when he exited.

Being mindful that as more and more people came into the pub their view of the men would become difficult to maintain, Chris suggested they should give up their table and find a better position. Sophie agreed, and they were barely out of their seats when the room plunged into pitch-black, unsettling darkness.

The sound of Christmas cheer, of laughter and excitement, came to an abrupt stop and gave way to a fearful silence. Then cautiously, as everyone reacted in their own time to the unexpected, did the inquisitive buzz of the crowd return. And as their confidence grew, so too did the good-humoured repartee and shouts to 'pay the bill' and 'get the lights on!' Temporarily unnerved but now believing that all was well, that no harm was lurking in the darkness, brought the breath of life back into the crowd. Back to the joyous and comforting sound of a Christmas gathering when, a sudden, enormous flash of blinding light followed immediately by an almighty, thunderous bang, shook the room, and sent people cowering to the floor.

Terrified screams, desperate shouts for help, crying and calling out to friends and loved ones pervaded the darkness. Disoriented and frightened, they had lost control of their senses, deaf from the blast and visually impaired by the flash, they surged as one enormous entity. First one way, then another, barging and pushing each other in an effort to find the exit, to escape and save themselves. In their panic, tables were toppled over sending glasses to smash on the floor, adding to the already perilous escape for those having fallen and been trampled underfoot.

Outside in the street, the comforting sound of sirens meant help was on the way. In the meantime, Spence's small team of officers were busy cordoning off the scene, and local bobbies working the Christmas market were collecting up customers running out of the pub and taking them to safety. Many found it difficult to see and were screaming that they'd been blinded. Others couldn't hear and were dazed, but all were in shock, struggling to understand what the hell had just happened.

Within a short space of time, the market had been emptied of shoppers, stallholders were told to abandon their stalls, and side roads had been opened up to the emergency services. Inevitably, the press was one of the first on the scene, but even they couldn't get close to the pub. It could be a bomb that went off, and if it was, there may be another. Nobody was going anywhere near it, and for Spence, not only had he lost the three targets, but he couldn't find his two officers either. They had not emerged from the pub and the picture painted by the survivors suggested that there were casualties. But until the all-clear was given, and that would be when, and only when, the bomb squad had done their stuff first, could the emergency services go in.

FIVE

Tuesday 11th December – 20:30

On a side road, a few minutes' walk from Crystal Palace Park sat two men in a black van. Under the cover of darkness, the make was not identifiable, but on the rear door was a sign informing all who were interested, that it was a hired vehicle. In the back of the van was a large plastic bin bag which held two black jackets for disposal, and alongside, slumped up against the side panel, was a man drifting in and out of consciousness. His ankles and wrists were lashed with yellow tie wraps, his mouth covered with grey duct tape, and his head rested on his hands as if in a praying position. He too was destined for disposal.

In the driver's seat, sat Don, a rotund forty-four-year-old ex-con with a gnarled face, and bad teeth who viewed serving a sentence as a badge of honour. Hence, he was a truly terrifying individual. He was capable of the most heinous crimes because he had nothing to lose. The passenger, Liam, a tender twenty-four and former cellmate was excitable. He was out in the world but knew nothing about it, having been incarcerated in one kind of institution or another since his early teens. He was immature, naïve, unpredictable, and very dangerous. Neither had the acumen to succeed on their own and will spend their career as hired help. But their lack of brain cells didn't affect how they swung a sledgehammer over someone's back or kneecapped a person with a crowbar. They were evil. They enjoyed their job and had no respect for human life. No wonder this man sat praying. He had no chance of survival once in the hands of these two. And this man was John Taylor. So, how did he get involved with these animals? It was surprisingly easy really.

It began when Taylor noticed a loophole in the accounting procedure at Darcy House. Up to that point in his life, he had always been honest, but life had taken a turn for the worse, and here was that chance, that opportunity to put things right. He began pilfering small amounts, just enough to see him through the month. It was easy, nobody had an inkling about what was going on, and no one would ever suspect him of stealing. He was reliable, trustworthy, everyone looked up to him. He was beyond suspicion. And this made it easy for him. That was until he became greedy.

The little bit here and there that nobody would notice became larger and larger amounts that would be noticed. His only way out as he saw it, was to steal even larger amounts and gamble with it. But he lost. And for several months he'd been gambling and losing, then betting bigger sums in the hope he would win it all back. Someone should have told him that chasing your losses never works. Has anybody ever heard of a poor bookie? No. This man just kept digging himself into a hole, until one day, when he'd diverted so many funds that he couldn't hide it anymore, he turned to a money lender, and that monster was Luke Williams. A self-made man peddling misery. Taylor got his money with no questions asked. Happy days he thought, that was until Williams needed a favour, and the option to decline was not available.

The assignment wasn't dangerous, but it was important, and with a filleting knife held to his throat, that fact he clearly understood. He was in no doubt that if he screwed up, it would have severe consequences for all concerned but especially for him.

He was instructed to sit at the bar in the Dog and Duck pub and watch the entrance for the arrival of Max, the landlord's brother. He would be carrying a box of whiskey that he would pass over the bar. At which point Taylor was to leave by the back door, tripping the MCBs as he passed through the passageway, throwing the pub into darkness. The man did well. It went off as planned, so why was John Taylor trussed up and about to meet his maker? Simple, as far as Luke Williams was concerned, he was out of favour, and out of time. His fate was sealed when he legged it from Darcy House. That was a stupid thing to do as it brought suspicion to him and almost ruined a job that was six months in the planning. Now, they had what they wanted, but he had to go. This little weasel will surely grass to save his skin, and this firm had more to do.

Taylor's low-level gurgling from a punch in the gut had increased in pitch as he became more aware of his situation, and Liam was irritated by it.

"Shut the fuck up!"

Don, concerned that someone would hear, told Liam to do the same.

"Why can't we just finish him now?" griped Liam. Like a wild dog, he had the scent of a kill and was baying for blood.

"We'll stop this prick breathing when the gaffer says we can." snarled Don. "Be patient, you'll get blood on your hands before the nights out."

Taylor could hear the conversation and was terrified. He didn't want to die. He didn't believe he deserved to die, and the fear of what was going to happen to him sent a surge of adrenaline coursing through his body. He had triggered the fight response which engulfed him with a potency befitting a warrior. He was determined to survive. His heart throbbed inside his chest as he threw himself against the side of the van, over and over again, causing it to rock violently.

"Turn it in, you useless piece of shit!" screeched Don. Who was being buffeted and splashed with hot coffee from a paper cup he held between his knees.

But Taylor continued with desperate intensity hoping that someone would notice and come to his rescue. Don had to stop him, but his bulk made scrambling over the seats into the body of the van a non-starter. Instead, he lumped out of his seat and hurried to the back. He scanned the area. He couldn't see anybody around and no curtains were twitching. Ham-fistedly he struggled to put the key into the lock, and when he succeeded, the rocking had stopped. Cautiously, he pulled the door a little way open. Taylor may have managed to free himself and he didn't want a broken nose if the door was kicked from the inside. But Taylor was no longer a problem. He had a bigger one, and it was called Liam, who sat, straddling Taylor, holding a boning knife to his throat.

"Let me shut the fucker up!"

Taylor was trembling and his eyes bulging in fear as he pleaded for his life.

Don slammed a fist onto the floor of the van,

"Not now! Williams wants this piece of shit alive! Now fuck off back to the front seat."

Liam waved the knife under Taylor's nose, then whispered in his ear,

"It's me you want to fear, not fucking Williams." A sick sense of empowerment etched across his face.

Don, whose responsibility it was to keep Taylor alive, was still shaking with rage as he hauled himself back into the driving seat. He couldn't believe what had happened. Wrongly, he had assumed that when he ordered Liam to stay put while he got out and dealt with Taylor, that he would obey. He should have known that the psychopathic kid couldn't be trusted to do as he was told, and now Don was concerned for his own mortality. He knew that Williams wanted Taylor alive. He had questions to ask. Important questions about Darcy House and Sammi Mancini. He also knew that Williams had no capacity for forgiveness. He would blame him if anything happened to Taylor, and Don would pay with his life for the failure. What to do now? He had to leave the scene, that was certain and drove off in the direction of Croydon where he could pick up the A23 to Haywards Heath, and to the safety of an old lags cottage until Williams got in touch. It would be empty now that his mate was admitted to a care home, and he knew where he hid the key.

Don was expecting the journey to be a stressful one. He would have to keep to the speed limits and not do anything that would attract attention from the coppers. If he got stopped with Taylor in the van, trussed up like a turkey, he would be banged up for sure and he wasn't ready to go back inside yet. He had plans, and the little shit sitting beside him was about to fuck everything up. As Liam became more and more frustrated with Don's careful driving, the atmosphere in the van became more and more tense, made significantly worse by Liam's reluctance to put the knife away. Don would have no way of protecting himself if Liam lashed out. He could imagine the knife being planted into his thigh, and it wouldn't matter to Liam that they might crash, the concept of consequence being non-existent in his mind.

21:00

Spence had arrived back at the station. He was mentally and physically exhausted, but before he could call it a day, he would need to attend a debrief. Assembled in the main office were colleagues that had attended the scene earlier and were familiarised with the situation, and those that were station based.

As expected, the home team had been kept busy handling requests for information from both the media, and family members of the victims, and the away team had done their best to keep them updated. Nonetheless, the public perception of how the incident was being handled was in negative territory, mainly because officers were still in the throes of investigating the bizarre incident and had little to go on.

DCI Fielding stood at the front of the room next to the incident board, and DSU Merriman sat with Spence at a table beside it. The atmosphere was uncharacteristically subdued, as for the majority, it had been a double shift, and fatigue was taking over.

"Firstly, and I speak for all of us." Acknowledging the senior officers around him. "Thank you all for your exceptional duty today."

Fielding was always considered to be a very genuine man, and his sincere address was not wasted on these officers. Backs straightened, and chins raised in readiness for what was to follow.

"After speaking with bomb squad officers investigating the attack on the Dog and Duck pub, I can confirm that a stun grenade, also known as a flashbang, was deployed. An investigation as to how it was acquired is being undertaken by a specialist team, but the reason it was used, we suspect, was to cause panic. Which it did. Thus, giving certain, as yet unidentified individuals, the opportunity to rob the place. I can also confirm that nobody died but a significant number were taken to the hospital presenting with a variety of injuries, including eye and ear conditions, fractured bones, and lacerations. However, the landlord, Bob Welch, and his brother Max were both bludgeoned in the attack and have been admitted for observation." At which point he paused and passed over to Spence.

"I'm pleased to report that neither Sparkes, nor Steele were seriously injured in the attack, and are currently being checked out at the hospital." A sigh of relief rippled around the room.

"As most of you will be aware, they had John Taylor under surveillance and had followed him into the pub. He positioned himself at the end of the bar and left, using the back exit, just before the stun grenade went off. We suspect he was the person responsible for throwing the pub into darkness, and I have no doubt that fingerprint analysis from prints taken off the MCBs will prove us right. Therefore, he must be considered a member of the firm that carried out this audacious crime. Unfortunately, he has not been located. Neither have the two men in black jackets that were also under surveillance, which we suspect were responsible for the stun grenade. These two men are of course also suspects in the death of Gemma Willis, and that of James Wilson, and resulting from images taken by Sparkes on his phone, one of the men has been identified as Donald Fallows." And placed his mug shot up on the board.

"The second man has not, but intel suggests that it's highly likely to be a known associate called Liam Frost." His mug shot was placed up alongside. "Both of these men should be considered armed and dangerous and an APW has been issued."

Sarah Bloom raised her hand,

"Do we know what was taken from the pub?"

Fielding opted to answer,

"That's a good question. As far as I can tell, the Dog and Duck is not that popular and in the most part their sales are paid for by card. They wouldn't have had a large amount of cash on the premises. Perhaps more than usual as it was a special occasion, but that still wouldn't be enough for a firm to devise and carry out such an elaborate crime. This was well-planned, organised and funded with the expectation of a big payday. So, why was this pub targeted is indeed the question. But we do have our suspicions."

Fielding handed back to Spence.

"From the witness statements taken so far, the last thing several people remembered before the lights went out, was the entry by Max Welch at about seven-fifteen, holding a white box. Nobody could remember what was written on the box, except that it was in red and gold print, but all agreed it was big enough to hold six full-sized bottles of drink. Max, however, denies he had a box, and after a thorough search, no item resembling the description was found. Therefore, it can be assumed that the box, which we believe held drugs was stolen. Sniffer dogs have identified the presence of drugs on the premises, and the most positive reactions were achieved in the following areas: on the shelf under the bar, in a cupboard off the kitchen, and in both the living room and the second bedroom upstairs, where a set of scales were also discovered. In view of this, I think we can confidently suspect that the landlord and his brother are dealers. And therefore, it's likely that the box held a delivery of drugs. If we're right, then the drugs will now be in the hands of the offenders, and our job is to work with the drug squad in the identification and detention of all members of this firm."

Fielding rose from his seat,

"The night shift has been briefed and will continue with the investigation. Tomorrow's another day. Get some sleep and we'll meet up again first thing for a report on the progress of the investigation, and to discuss how to proceed. DI Spence will also feedback on developments in the Gemma Willis and James Wilson inquiry."

SIX

Wednesday 12th December – 07:00

Darcy House sat in darkness. A cold, concrete pariah wrapped in police cordon tape. Even at this early hour, curious and intrigued members of the public with a taste for the macabre scuttled past, hoping to get a glimpse of something. Hoping there would be something to discover and relay to the family at dinner time. Something significant about the murder of the delinquent girl, the one who probably brought it on herself. However, they would be disappointed.

The action happened in the dead of night. It always happened in the dead of night, while they and others like them, were asleep in their warm beds. While they snuggled together in the safety of their perfect homes, safe in the thought that nothing bad would happen to them. The same very thing that Gemma had thought, and hoped for, when she entered Darcy House.

She thought it was a place of safety. She thought she could escape from the shepherd, the man who had made her life a misery. But this man appears to gain unchallenged entry everywhere. To have free reign over everybody with no questions asked, and to steal the spirit of young girls, with no questions asked. And now he had become even more demanding and pursued her relentlessly.

It had been just after midnight, that his henchman had made a stealthy approach through the rear gardens and armed with the security code, and key to the back door, had made an incident-free access into the property. They were instructed to head for the office and to search Taylor's desk in particular.

At twelve-forty-five, thirty miles away, Don and Liam were parked in woodlands. The plan was to bury the corpse of Taylor. This poor, unfortunate man had met a grisly death following a phone call from Williams informing the pair that he had no further use for him, and psychopathic Liam hadn't wasted any time carrying out the murder. Before the call had ended he had scrambled over the seat, held Taylor's head up by the hair, and sliced him open from ear to ear. His head fell forward, there was a gurgling sound and blood gushed out, splattering the roof, and spurting over Liam's sick smile of achievement. It flowed quickly, filling the ridges of the van floor where it moved at pace to form a well inside the door. It would be less than a minute before it dripped profusely out of the join and onto the gravel driveway at the cottage. Don tried desperately to mop it up with an old blanket he found in the back, but it was everywhere. His only option was to wait a while until it had congealed and clotted before he could drive away.

A toss of a coin determined that Don would start the digging, but after only a few shovels he'd been spooked by torchlight he thought he saw in the distance, and the dig was halted. He'd been caught as a poacher in the past, so knew there was a possibility that the woods were monitored for suspect behaviour. It wasn't a big deal, he just got a caution and a hefty fine, but being caught in the act of digging a grave would be a very different thing. And while he sat pondering his problem, a mere sixteen miles away, DI Spence was doing the same.

It was the second time that he'd got up and made himself a cup of camomile tea. He wasn't particularly fond of it but needed to sleep and thought it would help. His wife June, disturbed by his comings and goings in the middle of the night, was now wide awake too. For her, now that Milly,

Spence's niece, had been found safe and well, tonight was going to be the first good night's sleep she'd had in ages.

Spence placed his mug on the side table, sat on the edge of the bed and sighed. June leaned over and gently rubbed his back, "This case has really got to you, hasn't it?"

Spence, appreciating her thoughtfulness, laid back into the bed and scooped her up in his arms. His love for June saw no bounds. He adored her. June was Spence's happy place and today she would also be his listener, a job she took on from the outset of his career, and a good listener she was too.

It had been at a college prize-giving evening that the pair had first met. June was awarded her certificate of competence in hairdressing, and Spence, known just as Dave at the time, was a newly qualified bobby on a 'meet and greet the public' assignment.

Back in the day, it wasn't unusual for officers to attend local events, to get to know those that lived and worked on their patch. It doesn't happen now, there's just no time for that personal touch anymore, which could be one of the reasons that the public perception of the police has changed. Indeed, it is a topic to raise the pulse of many officers but particularly that of Spence.

When I first started, he would rant, youngsters had respect for the police and then launch into a litany of examples where the police are treated like the enemy. But tonight, he is focused on the job at hand, and putting the world to rights will need to take a back seat.

"I should be used to the evils of mankind by now," he said despondently, "and it's not as if I don't know that these people and these situations exist, but this little lass…" he sighed.

June not needing him to finish his sentence, she understood how he was feeling and what he meant. "Talk to me."

Spence gave her arm a loving squeeze, "I think this one's too disturbing, even for you."

"Try me. I'm a big girl now."

Spence thought for a moment, "Okay, I'll give you an outline of my problem, well one of them anyway."

"One of them?"

Spence laughed, "June, this case is getting more and more complex by the hour, and believe me, the problems are stacking up."

"Right. One at a time then. Hit me with it - the biggest one first?" she said playfully.

Spence chuckled, "My biggest one, my love, is that I don't spend enough time with my beautiful wife!"

She gave him a cuddle, then together, in readiness for the serious conversation, propped themselves up against the headboard.

"My second biggest problem is this. The bedding found on the bonfire belongs to Darcy House, and I'm sure that when the DNA analysis report comes in, we will find it was Gemma's bedding. The working assumption being that she was murdered in Darcy, wrapped in it, taken to the tracks and then it was put on the fire to burn along with her phone."

"Okay, and your problem is?"

"My problem June, is first, considering she was seen leaving Darcy on Thursday, how did she get back into the building without being seen? And second, how was she taken out without being seen? And I suppose that's two problems, isn't it."

"Possibly, if she was alive when she went in, and dead when she came out. But what if she was already dead? Then it becomes the same problem, doesn't it."

"So, you're thinking she was murdered elsewhere and then taken to Darcy?"

"It's possible, isn't it."

"Yes, it bloody well is, and now we have another problem."

"Which is?"

"Where was she murdered, and who by of course."

"Now, that *is* two problems," she said.

But her retort was lost on him. He didn't hear it. He was deep in thought. He knew from speaking with Sammi Mancini, that a daily meeting with staff and residents was held in the dining room at four o'clock, for fifteen minutes each day. That way even the kitchen staff could attend without anything being spoilt. She also made a point of mentioning that the main door would be shut for privacy, thus, allowing the residents and staff the freedom to say how they were feeling without being interrupted or overheard by strangers. So, it would be possible for Gemma to have been taken into Darcy at that time, but not through the main door, and by someone who knew the routine, and that man Taylor was rearing his ugly head again. Spence was sure he had something to do with it, and if, as he now suspects, she was brought to Darcy post-murder, then where would he have hidden her?

It would have to be somewhere out of sight of everyone else. Somewhere that nobody has access to, except perhaps, for one person, or possibly two. But where would that be? His head was beginning to ache as he strained to remember his tour of the property. Floor by floor, he systematically retraced his steps to recall the layout, what the room was used for and who was associated with it. He was hoping to have a brain wave, but unfortunately, it wasn't forthcoming. However, through analysis and deduction, he did reach a conclusion, and the longer he thought about it, the more credible it became, and triumphantly announced,

"Got it."

"Got what?" asked June. Who had now been unceremoniously abandoned as Spence leapt out of bed and was hurriedly pulling on his clothes.

"Dave, it's a quarter past two! Where are you going?"

"I have an idea June and I need to test it out. Go back to sleep and I'll phone you later," he called out. The words trailing off, indicating the speed of his descent down the stairs.

CID Office – 07:00

Spence had been busy since his arrival at three-forty-five. On his desk lay a forensic evidence bag, and alongside was a floorplan of Darcy House. In the past hour, he had been in a meeting with DCI Fielding, in which they reviewed all the information received to date and had organised the agenda for the briefing. He was feeling positive, and in no doubt, that today was going to see a turning point in the investigation.

Harris popped his head around the door, "Everyone's here sir."

Spence gave the thumbs-up sign, "On my way."

He met Fielding in the corridor, and they entered the main office together. Buoyant and confident, they presented a unified and positive presence. Fielding opened the briefing,

"Morning one and all. It doesn't seem five minutes since we were last assembled here, does it? But I hope you all managed to get some good rest."

And it has to be said that looking out into the sea of heads, it didn't appear that many could say they had. They were definitely lacking that freshly laundered, starched appearance and Fielding was aware of it, but he knew that the news from Spence, and that of their colleagues, would perk them up.

"Overnight, we have received reports from many of you, along with reports from forensics, and all will be read and discussed in this meeting." He then stood aside and handed over to Spence.

There is much to impart on all of the investigations, but

first I want to focus on Gemma Willis. Harris, can we hear your report on your interview with Jasmine Wright please."

Harris, not expecting to be the first one called to report, took a moment to retrieve the relevant papers from his file. Slightly flustered, he began,

"Jasmine said that she'd been texting Gemma on Thursday afternoon after she'd left Darcy House and Facetimed her in the evening. She said that her friend was having a good time, and had sent her a photo, but didn't reveal where she was, only that she was spending the weekend with her boyfriend, Sean McKinney. She also said that she'd tried texting her friend on Friday but had no replies and didn't have Sean's number."

"Have you a transcript of their text exchanges?" asked DSU Merriman. Who had just arrived following a meeting with the DCS.

Harris held it up, "Yes sir."

"And is there anything useful on it?"

"There is one text where Gemma says that it was Sean McKinney's landlord's car that picked her up from Darcy."

"But we don't know where he lives, is that right?"

"That's right sir, but we are working hard to trace him, and images of the room in which Gemma was standing when the photo was taken, when we do locate it, will confirm we have the right address."

"And what of the manager, Freddie Turner, what did he have to say for himself?"

Fielding spoke up, "I interviewed Mr Turner, and it appears he was due two days' holiday, Taylor had agreed to do his shifts, and he didn't know who made the arrangements. We've made enquiries into Watson's alibi, and everything checks out."

"And Taylor remains at large I take it?"

"Yes sir."

"Thank you." And nodded to Spence to continue,

"In view of the Facetime evidence, we can be confident that Gemma was alive at eleven-twenty, and forensics will concur with a time of death sometime on Friday. Therefore, it is unlikely that she was murdered in Darcy House. We know, because CCTV evidence proves it, that nobody resembling Gemma entered the property, at any time, on Friday."

He paused for a short moment, "However, I can prove that Gemma, was indeed present in Darcy House on Friday."

Everyone was intrigued and eager to hear what Spence had to say,

"Harris, get ready to read the bit in your report about when Jasmine returned to her room please." Then addressing the rest of the room, "And before he does that, let me fill you all in on the Darcy regime. Each day, they have a house meeting in the dining room, and everyone in the building attends."

At which point Spence pointed to the room on the Darcy floorplan he pinned on the whiteboard, clearly identifying its position to the right of the reception and the back door exit.

"Right. Go on lad,"

Harris cleared his throat, "Jasmine told me, that after the meeting finished on Friday, at about four-twenty, five minutes late because one of the boys kept moaning, that as she passed Gemma's room, she noticed that her bed had been stripped."

"Thank you. Anything else?"

"Only that she admitted to being the person who paid for Gemma's nails and that it was Sean McKinney who gave her the money, and who was waiting outside for her."

"Great, that's cleared that up, thank you. Did you ask her if she knew anyone called the shepherd?"

"I did, but she said no. However, she also said no when I asked if she smoked weed, and I know that's a lie, I could smell it on her clothes."

"Okay. So we need to speak to her again. Make the

necessary arrangements to do that and ask Sammi Mancini to be in attendance. Now, back to Darcy. In the twenty minutes that the meeting was being held, I believe that Gemma's dead body was taken to Darcy, wrapped in her bedding, and left in this room here." Where he pointed to a storeroom for flammables that has an external door into the rear courtyard.

"But that room was searched," stated Hearn.

"What was it searched for? What were they looking for? This lass was killed with a lethal injection. She wasn't bludgeoned – there'd be no blood."

And moving over to the desk, he picked up a small, clear evidence bag and held it aloft.

"In here is a little white button. It belongs to Gemma's blouse, and I found it in the storeroom.

That means she was killed elsewhere, brought to Darcy, and kept in that storeroom, wrapped in her bedding until she was collected on Saturday night and taken to the tracks. It also means that someone who either works at Darcy or is able to come and go freely, stripped that bed, and opened the storeroom for whoever brought her body into the building. My money is on Taylor, but inquiries are still ongoing. I can also confirm that CCTV picked up a black van, similar to a transit but as yet unidentified, drive to the rear of the building at five past four on the Friday. Unfortunately, the CCTV at the rear is not working, but I'm convinced they had Gemma in the van, and that it's the same van connected with the hit-and-run of the warden."

He paused for a moment to ask if there were any questions. Hearn raised his hand,

"Was there no CCTV showing the van arriving and leaving on the Saturday?"

"Unfortunately, a gremlin – again, probably named Taylor, put all CCTV out of action on the Saturday, so we have no proof of her collection prior to being dumped at the railway track. However, I have instructed officers to locate and retrieve all CCTV along the main road. If we can identify which direction it travelled to Darcy, we should be able to work backwards and see where it came from."

Sarah raised her hand, "Are we any closer to understanding why she was left at the tracks?"

"I can only suppose that whoever organised the disposal of her body, knew Gemma's situation and knew she was feeling suicidal."

"So, our eyes *are* on a professional then." Her brusque response raising a few eyebrows.

It had been a suspicion she'd had from the outset, and Spence knew it, but he was reluctant to make that leap from suspicion to certainty.

"It could be Sarah, and there's good reason to suspect it is, but it could also be an acquaintance, or God forbid, a friend. We must keep an open mind. However, it makes sense, doesn't it, to compile a comprehensive list of all professionals that had any dealings with Gemma, and to conduct a thorough background check on them."

"Yes, I believe it does." she replied firmly, omitting the required 'sir' from her reply, and with a hint of 'I told you so' in her tone.

"Then I'll leave that in your hands," he responded forthrightly. Knowing that she would not accept the assignment gracefully, she would consider that job as beneath her, and most likely give him the silent treatment for a short while, just long enough to make her feelings known. But sometimes she needed reminding of who was in charge, and this was one of those times.

"Now, Hearn, your report will fit in nicely here."

"Sir. I found that James Wilson, the warden, lived close by to Darcy House and that he did carry out odd jobs for them. Mainly drain clearance and weeding. But more importantly, I was contacted by the fire service, who told me that he was on their radar. Apparently, there are numerous reports made by officers regarding his presence at fire scenes. There's no evidence to suspect he started the fires, but they do believe he was fascinated by them. Considering his flat overlooks the wasteland where the bonfire was lit to burn the bedding and phone, then he could have seen who was responsible for it, and that made him a target."

"I think that's a very valid assumption. Well done, and any news on forensics?"

"It's coming in bit by bit. The identification of body fluids on the bedding has confirmed that Gemma's dead body was in contact with it. Human DNA not belonging to Gemma was also identified but as yet there is no match. They also found canine hair and are currently trying to ascertain what type of dog the hair came from, their assumption being that it was transferred from her clothes. The mobile was found to have no sim card and had been wiped back to default settings. Perhaps it was burnt to destroy any fingerprints."

"Could be, but nevertheless, that is a step forward, thank you."

Fielding took the floor,

"So, to sum up, we know how Gemma was killed, we now have a window of when she was killed, and we know where she was kept before being taken to the tracks. We've come a long way, but we still have a way to go. Our priorities are first, to find John Taylor. He is linked to the landlord that collected Gemma, suspected of hiding her body at Darcy, suspected of disposing the Darcy bedding on the bonfire, suspected of participating in the raid at the Dog and Duck, and it's highly likely that he will be able to identify the shepherd. Secondly, it's vital that we identify and trace that van, and thirdly, we need to find and apprehend Donald Fallows and Liam Frost. With all of that in mind, DI Spence will be speaking to you all after this briefing, to put you in teams and to hand out your orders."

"Where are we on the Dog and Duck investigation?" asked Merriman.

Fielding had taken the reins on this one,

"Tracking down the source of the stun grenade is in the hands of the bomb squad, and they will be keeping us updated," he said with confidence.

Merriman seemed less sure, "Make sure they do."

Fielding continued,

"The night shift has interviewed the majority of customers who had been taken to the hospital, but unfortunately, they had nothing new to add to our findings. Regarding the brothers, Uniform have arranged for a police presence during their stay in the hospital, which is expected to be for the next couple of days. On discharge, the brothers will be detained for questioning by ourselves, and the drugs squad.

"Do they know this?" asked Merriman.

"Yes, they do, and as expected, they have instructed a solicitor."

Then looking out into the room, Fielding identified DS Jake Madden and DC Fiona Wells,

"Both officers will be out today in the market area speaking with the traders and looking for possible CCTV evidence. I have also signed off on a public appeal for information, through a TV interview later this morning, and by incident boards in the market, and around the area."

"Good, and any news on forensics?"

Fielding shook his head, "Not yet, and it could be a long job, they have hundreds of fingerprints to check. I have asked them to work on the tables first, as we know that Donald Fallows was sitting at one, and confirmation of this will be beneficial, also we will be able to identify who was with him. We suspect it was Liam Frost, and hopefully, fingerprint evidence will prove that. We are also making enquiries at all known addresses in our search for the pair of them."

"Good. Sounds all in hand then," he said, with an air of authority befitting his status. And withdrew from the briefing.

The briefing then ended, and as everyone was filing out of the room, Spence pulled Fielding to one side. He was questioning the decision to include DS Jake Madden on the team dealing with the market investigation. Madden would certainly not have been Spence's first choice, but as Fielding was in charge of the investigation, he was out of the loop when decisions on staffing were being made.

These two men had a history. It was in 2014, that Madden, who at the time held DI rank in the fraud squad, headed up a joint initiative with Spence in CID. The aim of the operation, named Yellow Beak, was to identify and apprehend the ringleaders of a financial scam.

The criminal enterprise had over a period of three years, duped unsuspecting individuals into parting with their savings, in the belief they were being invested. Most, although very distraught, were able to come to terms with their financial loss. But two gentlemen, unable to cope with both the stigma of victimisation and the prospect of an impoverished existence in retirement, had committed suicide.

During the course of the investigation, they met a number of dead ends and the operation subsequently floundered. The lack of any progress, and with the cost of the operation spiralling, necessitated an enquiry into how the investigation was being managed.

It was discovered that two male suspects who had been arrested, questioned, and then released with no further action, were found to have been illegal immigrants. And subsequent enquiries further identified that full background checks on the two men had not been carried out. If they had been, it would have revealed that they both had previous convictions for fraud. Neither man was apprehended, and no charges were ever brought.

The responsibility for that landed squarely on Madden's shoulders, and along with complaints from officers citing bullying tactics, his chance of coming out unscathed from disciplinary action, was very unlikely. Inevitably he was stripped of his DI rank and demoted to DS. Whereas Spence was considered blameless and allowed to stay in post. A decision that rankled Madden at the time. The question is, has he been able to move on, or will he prove to be a thorn in their side?

His partner on this assignment, DC Fiona Wells, was also known to Spence, but for a very different reason. Before signing on, Fiona had worked for the force in an administration position and often assisted Spence. She was efficient, proactive, sensible, and extremely down to earth. She knew how Spence worked, knew how the CID office worked, and in many ways, had more experience and knowledge under her belt, than some of the other officers drafted in. With all this in mind, Spence's hope was that she'd be a positive influence on Madden.

Fielding listened but didn't share the same reservations, and was pushing ahead with his plans, leaving Spence no choice but to accept it, and hope it didn't end badly.

His attention now turned to issuing orders to his own teams. DC Sophie Steele and DC Chris Sparkes' job was to find the black van, and DC Harris and DS Bloom's job was to find Sean McKinney. Both getting a result would make Spence's day.

He in turn would be accompanying Hearn back to the warden's flat to confirm the line of sight to the bonfire. He would also be speaking with the man who put the fire out, and speaking with the other neighbours to ascertain if anyone else saw who lit the bonfire or saw James standing by it.

They will also be liaising with other teams, both off-site and station based, in the search for John Taylor. Spence's hope is that someone gets a lead on his whereabouts. He doesn't believe this man has disappeared and is convinced that he's hiding out locally and that someone must know where he is.

Seven

Wednesday 12th December – 09:00

Sophie was excited to be working with Chris again, although she hoped that it wouldn't be as eventful as the Dog and Duck fiasco. As a newbie, she was always analysing her performance, but felt good about the way she'd handled herself that night, and certainly won't be revealing to anyone, that she had a good cry when she got home. She was absolutely fine until that moment when she allowed herself to relax, and then it hit her, she could have been killed, and the tears flowed.

Today, she expected it to be a pretty safe, no fireworks, Sherlock Holmes type exercise. Researching, delving, checking, and arriving at conclusions. Sparkes, however, was not that type of copper. He liked to be out and about, sniffing around like a bloodhound. As it turned out, it was to be a bit of both.

Sophie sat at her desk and was scrolling through the information on her PC, while Chris sat beside her.

"You're going too fast," he moaned, "my eyes can't focus."

"There's not much to see yet, I'm just whittling down the parameters of the search."

"What parameters are you using?"

"Firstly, I put in vans, which brought up nearly four million in the UK."

"Blimey! Four million? Are you sure?"

"Yes, look," Spinning the monitor round for him to see more clearly. "And then I put in black, and then London."

The screen now showed two hundred and nine thousand.

"That's still too many. Where would we start?"

Sophie thought about it, "The problem is, we don't know which make of van it is. I could put in Transit and get a smaller number, but what if it isn't?"

"Okay, we have to do this another way. As far as I can see, we've got two real choices, either it was a van that is owned, or it was hired. But I doubt it was owned. Who commits a hit-and-run, and disposes of a body in their own van? Or come to that, even one borrowed from a friend, or a works van?"

"Yeah. They'd have to be really stupid. One look at the number plate and they'd be identified for sure." She then thought for a moment, "But what if they just changed the number plate?"

"That carries a risk of being caught by ANPR, doesn't it? And this lot are not risk takers."

"Yeah, you're right, I'm just processing it all. You know, thinking of all the angles."

Sparkes, confident now that Sophie was on board with his idea, continued,

"There we go, so we've eliminated thousands already. Now, secondly, if it was a hire vehicle, they wouldn't need to travel to the boondocks to hire it, because they wouldn't have used their real names. So, let's trawl all the hire firms in a ten-mile radius, and see if we can at least, get an idea of how many vans we're talking about."

Sophie agreed, "Sounds like a good plan to me."

At which point, Spence walked up to the desk,

"My advice is to check dismantlers first."

The pair looked at each other,

"Yes sir, that's just what we were thinking," replied Sparkes.

Sophie was stunned at his reply but knew to keep quiet.

"Good. If I was them, I'd think about getting rid of it as soon as possible, wouldn't you?"

"Absolutely sir." agreed Sparkes.

Sophie couldn't believe how easy it was for Chris to tell a bare-faced lie, and he was now slipping off that pedestal she'd had him on. Snubbing his efforts to explain, she pushed a list of dismantlers into his hand, and ordered him off. She would stay office bound and ring around the vehicle hire firms.

Meanwhile, Sarah and Harris were already on the road and making their way to Social Services. They had arranged to meet with Fergus Butler, the administrative coordinator. He had promised to look into McKinney's file and have the information ready for them when they arrive.

Sarah was sceptical. She'd had many dealings with them in the past, and nothing was ever available when promised. She was anticipating at best, a lengthy wait, one they could ill afford, and at worst, a statement confirming the loss of files.

To her surprise, Mr Butler was ready and waiting for them in reception. Considering she'd spent most of the journey bending Harris' ear about this cold and unfriendly organisation, she felt a little awkward when he welcomed her with an outstretched hand.

"It's not normally like this," she whispered to Harris. As they followed Mr Butler to his office.

They were shown to two chairs facing his desk and invited to sit down. Sarah thought he was likeable, and what she would call, a homely man. It could have been because he had a broad smile, and his salt-and-pepper beard was a little wild. But it was mainly because he wore an everyday, basic shirt and a cable knit cardigan. She also expected his wife would probably have made sure he had a clean hankie in his pocket too. She imagined that he was one of those men that spend most of his life in one job, who isn't particularly ambitious, and who only ever makes just enough money for his needs.

Harris didn't like his smile at all, he thought it was false, and especially didn't like his limp handshake, therefore arriving at the conclusion that Fergus was a creep.

He offered them a coffee, which they declined. It wasn't a social visit, they needed to hear what was in the file and get going.

Thumbing through the papers and shifting them into a different order, he seemed to be time-wasting and hesitant, as if he wasn't comfortable about speaking out,

"This boy, Sean McKinney, has been known to us for many years," he stated coldly and matter-of-factly. "His first placement at Darcy was in two thousand and ten when he was eight."

"And what caused removal from his home at such a young age?" asked Sarah.

"Home, if you can call it that, was a Lewisham squat. He was found hiding under the floorboards, and laying above him, was the dead body of his mother. Died from a drug overdose, as most of them do." His remark clearly identifying his prejudice towards those with drug dependency.

Sarah was not impressed by his 'them and us' view of society, nor with the tone of his delivery of the information. Where was the human element? Where was the empathy?

"Oh, that's an awful experience to go through, isn't it. No wonder the boy is troubled."

Butler responded with an obligatory, but clearly unaffected, "I suppose so."

"How long was he at Darcy?" asked Harris.

Butler fiddled with the pages again, huffed a bit, and then closed the file. He obviously knew this boy so well that he didn't feel the need to consult it.

"Not long. This boy was uncontrollable. Feral he was. Nobody could manage him. He was in and out of Darcy like a change in the weather."

Harris was getting frustrated, he wanted facts,

"Mr Butler, can you tell me exactly how many years he

stayed at a time please?"

"Years! Officer, it was never years. We were lucky if we held on to him for a couple of weeks at a time!"

Sarah was astounded, "He obviously had somewhere and someone else to go to. He was eight, after all, he couldn't survive on his own, could he."

"Well, I know it's hard to believe, but this kid did, and I can tell you how."

The pair listened, and Harris took notes,

"His mother had been a serial offender. Shoplifting since she'd been a nipper and trained him in the art of thieving as soon as he was able to walk, I expect. She would send him into a shop, and he would walk behind a couple, appearing to be with them, and all the time, he'd be filling his pockets. Of course, when the couple decided to leave the shop, the alarm would sound. As innocent people, they would stop and walk back inside to find out why, and the boy would keep walking."

"I'm sure I've heard about that scam before," commented Sarah.

"It's a new one on me," admitted Harris.

Butler leant forward as if to impart a pearl of wisdom,

"Lots of people have heard it before, but nobody recognises it in practice. This boy was able to look after himself very nicely, thank you. That was until he started to grow, and he couldn't get away with it anymore."

"Do you know what he turned his hand to next?" asked Sarah.

"Oh yes. It was drugs."

"And do you have any further information on that?"

"No. But, I often see him hanging about. Especially near the lockups behind the shops. I expect a dealer lurks around there."

"And have you seen him recently?"

"No, I've been on annual leave for two weeks, but if I see

him again, I'll let you know." Assuming they'd finished, he stood to show them out.

Sarah smiled up at him, "We do have a few more questions if you don't mind."

He glanced at his watch, implying they were keeping him from something, and regained his seat.

"Could you check your records for any mention of family members please?"

"I don't need to," he snapped, "the answer is none."

Sarah sensed his growing animosity towards them, but it wasn't going to stop her from asking all her questions,

"And what schools did he attend?"

"None." Came the short, impatient, and rude reply.

"None?" she repeated. Astonished and hoping she'd misheard him.

"That's right. None. He needed taming before mixing with other kids, but you'd have to trap him first, and nobody ever could."

Sarah found that hard to believe, and both of them were disgusted with his terminology for the boy, speaking about him as if he was a wild animal. She was upset with him, made obvious by the tone of her next question,

"And what professionals were involved in his lack of care and lack of treatment?" she demanded.

Butler's face turned red, and he was about to respond, when something held him back, choosing instead to give a disrespectful laugh as he begrudgingly opened the file. As he scanned the papers for the information, his sighing and grunting made it appear that they'd asked for the earth.

Sarah turned to Harris, "This is more like it." she whispered.

Harris gave a nod in agreement, "Perhaps we could just take the file and do the donkey work ourselves," he suggested.

This time, Butler didn't hesitate to reply, "I'll make a phone call." Then hurried out of the room.

"What's wrong with him?"

"I expect he's late for elevenses," quipped Sarah.

At this point, a young girl came in, picked up the file and told them that she would make them a copy of it. Then said that she wouldn't be long and that as Mr Butler was now needed elsewhere, she would show them out.

"Well, you weren't wrong Sarah, they definitely are a funny lot here."

Sarah agreed but was more concerned that the copy they'd been promised, would be a complete copy, and not one that Mr Butler had edited. She felt sure, that from the outset, he'd been engaged in damage limitation, and had no doubt that the file, in its complete state, would identify areas where the service had let the boy down.

Back at the station, Jake Madden and Fiona Wells were not experiencing the start they expected. For an hour, they had sat and plotted their route through the market and surrounding area, planned how they were going to conduct their investigation, and identified specific targets to question. But all that went to pot, when Fielding informed them that they would be working under the command of the drugs squad on an undercover operation. That type of investigation suited Jake down to the ground but had Fiona all of a tizz.

In her previous admin role, she'd seen officers in preparation for undercover work, and had grave reservations about her ability to act, and to remember all the background on whom she was playing.

"You'll be fine," assured Jake, "just follow my lead. If I think you're sinking, I'll step in."

That was okay for him to say, she thought, he had bags of experience, and with his line in patter, he'd fit in as a market trader with no trouble. However, although being down to earth, Fiona was a boarding schoolgirl, with an educated voice, and doubted her ability to pull it off.

They were directed to a room on the top floor, where they were introduced to the rest of the team. Fiona wasn't sure what to expect but didn't expect the majority of officers to be women, and now she was feeling better about things.

The aim of the investigation was to acquire evidence that the Dog and Duck brothers were dealing out of the pub and to identify other dealers working in the area. The intelligence suggested that a drugs war was emerging and that the incident at the pub would be the first, in a line of attacks, designed to eliminate any and all competition. The name in the frame as being the mastermind behind it was Luke Williams.

Under the guise of a businessman, breeding and racing greyhounds, Williams was able to conduct a lucrative criminal enterprise. But as it stands, charge and conviction for this man, are just words. It seems that whenever the police get close, witnesses go deaf, dumb, blind, or suddenly meet with an accident. It was understandable then, that although he doesn't have a warrant out for his arrest, that he should be considered armed and dangerous, and also to be mindful that he is the employer of many an unscrupulous thug.

It was decided that a new stall popping up on the market, at a time when a police investigation was taking place, would raise suspicion. Therefore, as Jake held the rank of sergeant, he was considered to have the demeanour and presence required to be a new market inspector, thus, giving him the opportunity to speak with all the traders. Two other male officers would act as council workers, sweeping, clearing, and of course, listening and chatting. It was these two officers that were in charge, and all the actors would be required to report to them.

The remaining four women and Fiona would-be shoppers, with the instruction to only pay in cash. They didn't want anyone being traced through their debit cards. Their orders were to simply keep their eyes open and report anything suspicious.

The briefing ended with a request to leave all personal effects, including anything with an address on it, and anything pertaining to their role in the police, in a secure box. These could be retrieved on return to the station. The women were then handed a purse, and on opening hers, she saw a £20 note tucked inside. Her look of surprise prompted Karen, one of the other officers, to comment,

"Twenty quid is amazing, it's normally only a fiver."

"But it's not possible to spend all day shopping at the market with only twenty pounds." she insisted.

"That's the thing," chuckled Karen, "try not to spend any of it." And handing her a scrunched-up carrier bag, asked, "Do you have a scarf you can do without?"

"Yes I have." Pulling it out from under her coat.

"Great, stuff it in this bag, and carry it about. It will look like you've bought something."

Fiona was bewildered and found it hard to get her head around it all.

"Spend what you need to but remember to leave enough for your bus fare." advised Karen.

"Bus fare?" she exclaimed.

Karen was astonished by Fiona's naivety, "There's no car sent out to pick you up when you're undercover. It's the bus for all of us."

And as a seasoned officer, she was concerned at the lack of preparation, and training, that Fiona had been given before being seconded onto the operation. She would need to keep an eye on her.

For Fiona, the seriousness of the operation was now very evident. And considering all the information, especially the latest from Karen, she was well aware that she'd have to keep her wits about her; think carefully about her every move, whom she spoke to, and about every word she uttered.

Don Fallows was also having to think about his every word. Liam, who had spent the night snorting cocaine and watching porn, was now coming down, and acting a prick. The boy was highly agitated, and Don knew that aggression and stupidity would follow. He couldn't afford for Liam to lose it. He needed him to be calm and quiet while he thought about a way out. The police would surely be on their tail by now, and so too Williams, he wouldn't want these two reprobates caught; they knew too much, and he would want them both silenced. But as far as he could see, there were only two ways he could achieve it. He either fed Liam's drug habit by banging more Charlie up his nostrils, thereby keeping him high and compliant, or he killed the bastard. The second option was not only a lot cheaper, but it would also set him free of the prick and give him a better chance at freedom.

He knew that the longer he stayed at the cottage, the bigger the chance of being found. And the more he turned it over in his mind, the more he became convinced that the only way forward was to go it alone. He would kill Liam and drop his body along with Taylor in the cesspit. But one thing he knew for sure, he wouldn't leave him lying around for a while, as they had with Taylor's body. The stench as he melted in the van was fucking criminal, and he doubted that he'd ever get rid of it. And whilst he had the van in his thoughts, he could think about where it could be dumped after he got to the coast, the plan being to get over to France, and then on to Spain, where he had associates.

Standing with his back to the window, Don watched as Liam pulled a baggy of cocaine from his jean pocket and chucked it on the table. Then winced at the screech, as the mindless addict dragged his chair over the flagstones and up to the table, all the time whinging that he wanted food. And with the news that there wasn't any, proceeded to vandalize the wooden tabletop with a long blade flick knife. The monotonous note of the stabbing was interrupted only by the spasmodic need to scratch at his body. Don realised that he was coming down fast and that he would need to act quickly. It was now, when Liam was slow and vulnerable, that he needed to make his move. If he let him use the cocaine beside him, it will be too late, Don would have missed his chance; he was no match for Liam when high, his youth, his strength and his knife skills would win out. He also knew that his hefty bulk would not enable him to make a surprise attack. He would need to disable Liam, before he could kill him.

Turning around to face the window, he checked his pocket for the electrical cord he'd harvested from a table lamp the previous night, then sliding his hand into the sink, grabbed the hilt of a sharp kitchen knife that lay in wait.

Liam had now reverted to stabbing his blade into the tabletop and gouging out deep channels, his free hand laid flat on the surface. Don could see Liam's reflection in the window, he was deeply preoccupied - the time to make his move was now. With a tight grip on the knife, he launched himself at Liam, and with immense force, plunged the knife into his hand, impaling it to the table. Liam screamed out in agony! His eyes bulging in disbelief as his fingers convulsed, splattering blood every which way. Squealing like a suckling pig being slaughtered, he attempted to pull the knife out, but Don had arrived behind him and slung the cord around his neck. With the ends wound around his hands, he pulled hard. Liam clawed at the cord with his free hand but made no impression. He gasped for air, his legs thrashed, and his body writhed as he struggled to free himself, but Don pulled the cord tighter and tighter, his knuckles white with the effort. Deeper and deeper it cut into Liam's neck, until his face turned blue, his arm slackened, and he fell to his knees on the floor. Don, who never left anything to chance, grabbed the flick knife, and planted it deep into Liam's back, giving it a twist at the end for good measure. Now he was sure the boy was dead.

EIGHT

Wednesday 12th December – 13:30

Spence had arrived back at the station to news that the black van had been identified on CCTV. On a previous occasion, when they'd attempted to track the van leaving Darcy on the Friday, the number plate had been obscured, and then after time, the van was lost in heavy traffic. But on Saturday, after leaving Darcy House, the van had been involved in a minor collision with a motorcyclist at a traffic light, and because the van failed to stop, the biker took their number. It was only when he reported it to the police a few days later, following the insistence of his insurance company for a case number, that CCTV evidence confirmed a match. Unfortunately, the number belonged to a 2016 Transit Custom, reported stolen the week before.

On hearing of the development, Sophie just shook her head, so much for Chris' conclusions about number plates. However, they now knew the type of van they were looking for, and she rang Sparkes immediately to relay the news. But as the Transit Custom had been the biggest-selling van of the year, for several years, neither of them felt like they'd made any progress at all. The task had just got bigger. However, Spence updated the bulletin to inform all officers of the type of van to look out for.

It was certainly the correct course of action to take, but it will turn out to be only luck, and an inquisitive officer, which stopped it from being a decision that would see an offender get away with murder.

In Haywards Heath, a traffic car had stopped a small

pickup following a prolonged attempt to attract his attention. It was only when they had no choice but to light themselves up and put the sirens on, that the driver sussed who had been flashing him, and put his phone down. He had no doubt at this point that he was in big trouble, and pulled into a garage forecourt, alongside the air pump.

It was in this garage that Don had decided to get some diesel, just enough to get him to the coast and was standing in the queue to pay. There were three customers before him when the police car pulled in. From his position, he didn't see the pickup, and assuming they were after him, left the queue, ran to the door, and hurried to the van in an effort to escape.

At this point, the police had absolutely no interest in his van, after all, they were looking for a Transit Custom, and a fairly new one at that, not an older, black Nissan Panel van. It was the cashier, blasting out on the Tannoy, that pump number six was leaving without paying, that drew their attention.

In his panic, he slipped on some spilt diesel, fell backwards, hitting his head on the concrete and was easy picking for the police. They assessed him as walking wounded and placed him in the back of their car. The intention was to drop him into casualty, check on his head wound, and then interview him at the station regarding the theft of the diesel.

But that all changed when the garage owner asked for his van to be moved off the pump. The officer sat in the driver's seat and was immediately met with the foul smell of death. Being familiar with the putrid stench, he thought he might be a poacher and could have had game rotting in the back. But after parking it up and deciding to have a look at the body of the van, the blood spatter and fibrous material on the panels and roof, was enough to know that more than game had been slaughtered in there. Reinforcements were called, forensics was summoned, and the garage closed for business.

Fallows did indeed spend some time in casualty, and the wait for attention wasn't a problem to him, he was in no hurry to leave. He knew that once that cell door closed, he wouldn't experience freedom again for a very long time, if at all. An opinion shared by the officers, and therefore, understandably assumed that his quiet, beaten demeanour, portrayed a man who had accepted his destiny behind bars. But it wasn't being locked up that caused his heart to beat faster, and his hands to be clammy with sweat, it was the belief that once Williams heard he'd been nicked, that he would be coming after him, and prison walls were no deterrent for this maniac.

Meanwhile, parked up at McDonald's, Sarah and Harris were scrutinising the contents of McKinney's file while lunching on Big Macs. They both agreed that the terminology used was ambiguous, and Sarah identified a serious lack of substantive reasoning in the decision-making. Worse still, it lacked any information on recent contacts or addresses.

"We have absolutely nothing to go on," despaired Harris.

Sarah shrugged, "Okay, we'll have to do it the hard way then. Let's go back to the beginning."

Harris looked bemused, "Am I to assume you mean visiting the only address we have here, the one where they found him in two thousand and ten?"

"I do. It's as good a place as any, and anyway, it's the only one we have."

Harris looked at his watch, "It's going to take over an hour to get there."

"Yes. And?"

"And an hour to get back, plus possibly an hour or two to find someone who remembers him, if at all."

"Harris, what is your problem? Will you turn into a zombie when the clock strikes six?"

"Huh! If only! If I miss my psyche appointment, what I'll

turn into, is a beat cop!"

Sarah felt awful, "Blimey, I'm sorry Harris. I didn't realise it was today." And reached into her pocket for her mobile, "I'll sort it. Is it Peggy Middleton?"

Harris nodded. His serious face evanesced as his oppo drew on her rank, to inform and emphasize how Harris' presence was essential to the investigation and therefore necessitated a need to reschedule. Witnessing her performance, it was even more important now that he got his career back on track, he wanted the clout that she just wielded.

Back on track, it did indeed take an hour to get there, and as you might expect, the squat was now a stylish property converted into six flats. It didn't come as a surprise to either of them, but it was disappointing, nevertheless.

Harris began to organise his briefcase and leaned over to the back seat for his coat. Sarah decided to read through the file again, and looked up,

"Where are you off to?"

"It's door-knocking for us, isn't it?"

"Yes, but I think we should knock on the estate agent's door first, he's bound to know something." Drawing Harris' attention to the agent's advertising board pinned to the front of the building that showed an address close by.

And her instincts were right. They found a member of staff who had been involved in the refurbishment and subsequent rental of the apartments, and although he didn't have any useful information on Sean McKinney or his mother, he did remember the day they were found.

He said that when the police searched the squat, they also found a young man in the basement. At first, because he was so cold, they presumed he was dead, but a doctor examined him and found a faint pulse. He was diagnosed with hypothermia. He survived and now runs a homeless shelter in New Cross, he may be able to help you. His name is Jess

Bower. At last, a lead, things were looking up for them.

When they arrived, two old age, homeless souls were sitting in the reception waiting to be seen. Jess Bower was in the office and could be heard telling someone that pets were not allowed.

"But it's my support ferret," came the pleading from a weary-voiced woman.

"Not in here Rosy," was his emphatic reply. "You're welcome but not the ferret."

"You're just a mean old cunt!" she screeched.

"Yes, I know Rosy, and a little less of the old please." And with that, marched her past everyone and led her outside and onto the pavement.

He returned to reception with a broad grin, and pulling his sleeves up to his elbows looked ready for action,

"Looks like it's going to be a busy night!" he announced.

"Yes, indeed," giggled Sarah, who found the whole interaction amusing.

"I can't imagine you two need a room," he joked, with a twinkle in his eye and a wink to Harris.

"No, we just want information please," explained Sarah. Presenting her ID.

"No problem officer. How can I help?"

Harris drew his attention to the two old men, who were craning their heads to hear, and asked if they could talk somewhere private. He showed them to a side room, and Sarah opened up the questioning,

"We understand that you were living in a squat in Lewisham in two thousand and ten."

"Yes, that's right. I was, and I bet you're going to ask me about Sean McKinney?"

"I was. How do you know?"

"Because you're the second person in as many hours interested in my past, or should I say Sean's present."

"Who was the other person?" asked Harris.

"I assumed it was a copper, like yourself. He didn't give a name, and thinking about it, he didn't offer up any ID either. Mind you, I was rushed off my feet, and he… he just looked the part. You know." He added, in an attempt to justify his lack of due diligence.

"No. I'm afraid I don't." came Sarah's frosty reply. "Can you describe him? Or better still, have you got CCTV here?"

"No, sorry. No funds for that." Then rubbing a hand across his bald head, he thought for a moment, "I reckon about six feet four. Had short, greyish, wispy hair, and wore a black suit. Oh, and he had a harelip thing going on. It wasn't severe, but you could notice it."

"Okay, thank you, and what did you tell him?"

"The same as I'm telling you, that Sean drops in here from time to time. You know, for a catch-up and stuff."

Harris threw a glance at Sarah. Did they both think the same? Sean popped in when he either wanted to buy drugs or wanted to sell drugs, the rolling papers Harris saw on the side suggested Bower may be a user.

"But the best person to speak to if you want to find him, is Barney, their like blood brothers those two. He lives in a squat near Putney Common. I don't know the address, but I can give you directions."

"Did you give the other man directions too?"

His embarrassed, 'penny just dropped' expression needed no words to confirm that he had.

Back in their car, Harris was looking online for a route, and Sarah sat scratching.

"I'm sure I picked up something from that ferret!"

Harris laughed, "I doubt that very much, they're clean creatures. I'm not too sure of the owner though." Then with a tap on her arm, assured her, "It's all in the mind."

"I bloody hope so." she cried. "But at this moment it feels

like it's all in my shirt!"

At which point their attention was drawn to a knock on the window. It was Bower. Sarah wound it halfway down, and he peered into the car,

"I forgot to mention that he was driving a white Mercedes."

19:30

Following the report on their findings, and the realisation that there were a good few hours of work ahead of them, Fielding passed the investigation over to the night shift. A decision that left Sarah and Harris disappointed as they wanted to see it through, but a decision that made a certain DC Peter Hearn very happy indeed. This would be his first step back into what he called, proper policing, and he didn't mind which team he was on, he would be out of the office.

Blue team would be sent out to investigate, and interview, anyone who may have seen the white Mercedes parked up at the homeless shelter. And Red team were to visit the Putney squat in their effort to find McKinney. The officers in this team having the greater experience and are more familiar with the requirements for this type of operation.

The officers assembled for the briefing. Fielding began by passing on intelligence received from the local station. It provided a good insight into who frequented the squat, and whether or not they were considered dangerous. For the most part, they were homeless people with substance abuse problems, but two of the squatters, Jodie Gash, and Barney Miller, were known to the police. They both had records for shoplifting and Miller had also been arrested for assault, attacking a fellow squatter with a knife, leaving him partially blinded. But the lack of evidence, and witnesses, had seen the charges dropped and his release back onto the streets, back to the squat that he ran like a military operation.

It was Miller, responsible for the barricades, that caused extensive damage and destruction to the building. It was Miller, responsible for the spate of local shoplifting, and petty crime, that kept his troops nourished and compliant. It was Miller, responsible for arming them and teaching them how to stand and defend against the bailiffs, and it was Miller that the team needed to apprehend and question, he would know where McKinney was, and they could clear the squat at the same time.

The operation would commence with surveillance, and the go-ahead for storming the building would be given when the presence of Miller was confirmed. Hearn had managed to secure his place on the red team, his intimidating presence being instrumental in the decision to include him. Needless to say, when Fielding gave the instruction 'no heavy-handed stuff unless you are protecting yourself', he was looking directly at him. Fielding, being ever mindful that he was taking a risk including Hearn, but he had little choice given the number of officers at his disposal, and Hearn, being ever mindful that if he let the bully out to win the fight, he would find himself fighting for an even bigger cause: his career.

By ten-fifteen, the team were in position, and waiting for instructions. Fielding sat in an unmarked squad car with Hearn. The atmosphere was tense. Neither wanting to open up a discussion, and both experiencing the rise in adrenaline with each call on the radio.

"A light can be seen in the ground floor front room, and one in the rear first-floor room overlooking the conservatory," announced one of the team.

"Copy that. Any movement?"

"No sir. Nothing yet."

They'd been in position for over an hour, and Fielding was getting frustrated.

"Hearn, walk down the street and let me know what you can see."

"Yes sir," he replied. Surprised that he chose him, but pleased to have the task and began exiting the car.

"Remember Hearn, you're just observing, and don't make it obvious."

The house was positioned further down the street on the opposite side of the road, and in his opinion, the numerous parked cars would have obscured his view, and decided to cross over.

Fielding was furious, and made his feelings known over the radio, for all to hear,

"I said don't make it obvious! Nobody walks past the house. Not even the neighbours, they all bloody cross over to this side to avoid it!"

"I know what I'm doing sir."

"I bloody hope so… Everyone be ready to move!"

Hearn knew that the team were listening to their exchange, and now, more than ever, he needed to get it right.

For a popular street in a dense residential area, it was surprisingly quiet. There was very little traffic and next to no one walking about. Perhaps the cold weather was keeping everyone at home. As he approached the squat, he was aware of voices, although he couldn't quite place them until he was practically on top of it. He knelt down pretending to tie his shoelace and could hear what sounded like an argument. As he fiddled with the lace, the disgruntled voices got louder, and exchanges became aggressive. All was not well in that house.

"There are people arguing sir, and the voices appear to be coming from the rear of the property."

"Are you sure Hearn?"

"Yes sir. Positive. There's definitely a confrontation taking place, and I'm sure I heard someone tell Barney to calm down."

Fielding, now confident that Miller was inside, decided that while the occupants were at each other's throats, it would be a good time to act, and gave the go-ahead. Within seconds, officers had wielded the Enforcer battering ram, and the front door was detached from its hinges but refused to yield, its passage to the floor being obstructed by breeze blocks stacked one upon the other behind it. Four officers were now up against the door, pushing and heaving, and gradually they managed to push the blocks aside, allowing further officers to run in.

"Police!" they shouted, "Police!" And armed with CS gas and Tasers, they barged into every room looking for squatters. Several were found where they lay in moth-eaten blankets on the floor, in drug or drink stupors, and oblivious to what was going on around them. Others, their bodies weakened by their addictions, put up a pathetic and futile resistance, while some, more energetic and wilier, took flight into the street. But one, in particular, stood his ground. It was Barney Miller, in his bohemian battle dress, standing in front of Jodie Gash, who sat whimpering in the corner of the kitchen behind him. In one hand he held an open flick knife to the throat of a young, uniformed officer. In the other, the scruff of the officer's neck.

Hearn was the first to encounter Miller, and with a taser in hand, bellowed at him to drop the knife.

Miller was in a state of panic and yelled at the top of his voice,

"You come near me, and I'll slit his throat!"

Fielding and two more officers had now arrived in the kitchen and sensing that Miller was overwhelmed at their presence and was unpredictable, he ordered them to leave. It was now just the four of them, and Fielding knew that he had to take Miller's mind off the officer. He pointed to Jodie.

"Let the girl leave. She looks terrified." And noticing blood on her feet, "Look, she needs medical assistance. Let her leave." he urged. Hoping Miller would put her welfare before his crusade.

But his cause was far more important,

"She's fine with me! I know what's best for her!"

He didn't. He didn't know what was best for either of them and like a frightened rabbit, skittish, agitated and trembling, he looked vulnerable and dangerous. His inability to get control of his involuntary shaking, caused the blade to nip at the officer's skin. Blood poured out of the wound, and a crimson river flooded down the front of his shirt. The young, inexperienced officer, not expecting to be in such a predicament, fainted. The knife slicing through his chin as he fell, and then landing awkwardly up against Hearn's legs, knocked Hearn off balance. It had taken them all by surprise, but for Miller, he'd lost his bargaining chip, and in a split second had grabbed Jodie up off her feet, using her instead as his escape route.

"I'll give it to her!" he shouted. Holding the tip of the knife under her chin.

"No. You won't." said Fielding, "She's special to you. Remember."

Miller now desperate to escape, twisted and turned, backing up as they inched their way closer to him.

"Get back! Get back! Or I will do it, I will!"

Jodie was in tears and terrified that he just might, "Please, Barney! No!" she sobbed. "Please, No!"

"Listen to her man. It's not worth it. A life behind bars is not what you want."

"I won't be behind bars! I'm leaving and taking Jodie with me!" he shrieked. "Get out of my way!"

Fielding pulled back, and spoke calmly,

"You're not going to escape. Even if you do what you've threatened, you'll be stopped before you get to the street.

There are a dozen armed officers out there. It's a no-brainer. Put the knife down. It's over. Put the knife down."

Miller's demeanour had now changed, the cocky, defiant warrior replaced by an anxious, distressed, and disturbed individual. He knew he was beaten but was afraid to give in, and at the moment he loosened his grip on Jodie, Hearn set off his taser, bringing Miller to his knees.

In the immediate aftermath of the raid, the paramedics attended to the young officer and took him off to the hospital. The squatters had been rounded up, and after identifying that McKinney wasn't amongst them, were ferried to the local station. Jodie Gash was being treated for shock and sat in an ambulance waiting to be collected by her tormented parents. She would be questioned later the following morning. Miller had been assessed, given a clean bill of health, and now sat restrained in the back of a squad car. He wasn't on route to the station yet. Fielding had questions to ask about McKinney, and he wanted the answers now.

This was the boy they needed, he would be the one to shed some light on Gemma's death and hopefully lead them to the shepherd. He also wanted to ask him about the white Mercedes. The blue team leader told him that the car was identified on CCTV and was registered to Robert Mann. However, they subsequently found that he had been in prison for the past three months, and could not have been the driver, either that evening or on the day Gemma was picked up from Darcy House. The owner of the vehicle would be interviewed at the prison in the morning, but now, his only option was to speak to Miller about it.

Fielding opened the rear door of the car and squatted down beside him.

"What can you tell me about Sean McKinney?"

"Don't know who that is." came the testy reply.

"Yes, you do." insisted Fielding.

"I told you, I don't! Now, fucking leave me alone!"

"Be assured my man, that is one thing I won't be doing. I will be in your face for as long as it takes to get some fucking answers. You can keep up this Che Guevara crap if you like, but I can see right through it, and so will your cellmates." he goaded, "if it's the attention you crave, then you're going to get a lot of it inside."

"Shut the fuck up!" he squealed.

"Nope. Not, till I know where I can find McKinney?"

Fielding's tenacious and immovable attitude was very evident and overwhelming to this wretched and defeated cavalier. His thoughts now focused on self-preservation.

"And what's in it for me?"

"Peace and quiet, my man. And if your information proves to be useful, I might put a good word in for you. Don't forget you have assaulted an officer. They'll come down hard on you for that."

Miller hung his head low. He was thinking about his options.

"Can you get me a cell on my own?"

"Depends."

"On what?"

"On your answers to my questions."

Miller couldn't get the thought of being hounded by other prisoners out of his head.

"I'm not a fucking pretty boy, I want your assurance that I'll have my own cell."

Fielding was unmoved,

"What do you have?" he asked. In a manner implying a deal had been struck, that he would get the boy a cell to himself. All the time knowing he had no clout to do anything of the sort. But he needed that information.

Reluctantly, Miller gave it up, “He camps out on the common.”

“Where on the common?”

“In the woodlands. Ask the local coppers, they’re always moving them on.”

“And who drives the white Mercedes?”

Miller looked up in surprise, “What?”

“The white Mercedes, who drives it?”

“I can’t tell you that. Really, I can’t. All I know is that it belongs to someone Sean works for now and then.”

Miller didn’t hesitate with his reply, held eye contact and his voice was steady. Fielding’s instinct was that he’d told the truth,

“And that work was something to do with drugs I expect, was it?

Miller nodded.

“And you’ve never met him?”

He hesitated before answering, “He came round the squat tonight.”

“When? What time?”

“About an hour before you. He asked about Sean,”

“What did you tell him?”

Miller looked sheepish and uncomfortable.

“Come on! What did you tell him?”

“I said he could find him on the common. Well… he was splashing out the spliffs, I thought he was all right!”

Fielding sighed in dismay, “Okay, what did he look like?”

Miller thought for a moment, “He was about six feet tall I suppose, taller than me anyway, and stunk of curry. I fucking hate the stuff.”

“Keep focused Miller,” demanded Fielding. “Clothes. What was he wearing?”

“Black trousers and a grey shirt.”

“Not a black suit?”

"He wasn't wearing a jacket, but it could have been."

"And hair colour? Facial features?"

"I remember he had dark hair, cut really short. He was very pale, but then most druggies are. Oh and he had a bit of a harelip."

"Did he say why he wanted Sean?"

"I expected he wanted to sell some stuff or something."

Fielding called one of the officers over and ordered him to organise house-to-house, and to request all CCTV if it captured the squat and the road."

"Okay, and what about the shepherd? Who is he?"

Miller's eyes flashed on hearing the name.

"You've gone quiet. This is not the time to go quiet. Is it?" suggested Fielding, his sarcastic tone implying he needs to give it up or Fielding will give up on him. "Come on, what do you know?"

"I don't know him, but…"

"But what?"

"Sean does."

"How does he know him?"

Miller reeled back in frustration, "You'll have to ask him. Really, I don't know. All I can tell you is that Sean said he was top-drawer bad and was terrified of him."

It was now vital that they find McKinney before the man in the white Mercedes, and every available officer was sent to the common. If the man was the shepherd, as Fielding suspects, then he already had a head start on them, and they needed the boy alive.

Coordinated and purposeful, the officers moved through the trees towards the lamplights that seemed to hover in the darkness. The copious amount of woodland litter underfoot made it impossible to execute a stealthy approach, ultimately alerting their targets to their presence before they had a chance to pounce. The flutter of tent flaps being opened, and the flash of heels caught in their torchlight as the occupants made their escape in the darkness, sent officers every which way trying to round them up. In the end, the number of tents abandoned was far more than those individuals captured and left just a handful to interview.

Fielding had them sitting in a row, and called them over one at a time to ask if any had seen Sean McKinney. Some were keen to help as long as no charges were brought but had nothing to offer. A couple, who wanted a warm bed for the night and a free breakfast, said they had seen him, but when pushed to describe him, were caught in a lie, and sent on their way. Fielding was frustrated and about to leave empty-handed when an officer approached. He reported that he'd come across a couple of tents, about fifty metres down the track, and in one of them he'd found a body. He said that he'd secured the site and had notified the pathologist and forensic team.

They arrived to find a small, green pop-up tent, barely noticeable tucked between the bushes. The zip flap had been opened. Fielding peered in, aiming his torch at the floor, and laying in a prone position on a grey sleeping bag, was the body of a male.

"Has anyone checked for signs of life?"

"Yes sir. He is dead."

"What injuries does he have?"

The officer looked perplexed, "Actually none, sir. He's all in one piece and there's no sign of any struggle. We think he probably overdosed. There are track marks on his arms."

Fielding let out a sigh of frustration, "Bloody hell!" And pulling the ID photo of McKinney from his pocket, he checked the face of the young victim and confirmed it was Sean. The boy was dead, and now, unless forensics offer up something to go on, so was his trail to the shepherd.

"Was he wanted sir?"

"Very much constable." came the dispirited reply. "Very much indeed."

NINE

Thursday 13th December – 07:00

DCI Fielding stood at the front of the room looking shattered. He was now well into his twenty-eighth hour without sleep, and it showed. For the past two hours he'd been scrutinising all the information he amassed to date on the shepherd and believed he'd identified a possible suspect.

Sitting alongside him were DI Spence, DSU Merriman and DCS Black. Before him, sat the day shift, looking significantly more alert than their counterparts, having just handed over before signing off.

"Thank you all for attending and thank you for all your effort. It has not gone unnoticed, and we are all extremely grateful."

This appreciative opening, a sure sign to the assembled who had experienced it before, that Fielding was setting them up for a lengthy meeting. And they were right. There was a lot to report on, a lot to discuss, and a lot of work to hand out to each of them.

"Yesterday, our enquiries led us to Putney Common, where the dead body of Sean McKinney was found, and following examination by the pathologist, I can confirm two things. Firstly that he died of a Fentanyl overdose, and secondly, he too had contracted Chlamydia. The pathologist believed he had been infected for some time. We, therefore, have good reason to also believe that he was the person who transmitted the disease to Gemma Willis. As it stands, we do not have a prime suspect for his murder. However, what we do have, is a possible suspect in Luke Williams, a person already being investigated for his part in the Dog and Duck raid. And with regards to that, we understand that Donald Fallows, who has been charged with the murder of Liam Frost and James Taylor, following the discovery of their bodies in the cesspit at a property in Haywards Heath, has admitted to setting off the flashbang. And he may well, with the right inducement, give Williams up as being behind it. He certainly has the money and resources to set it up, but is he also a murderer? Our investigations suggest he may well be, and in this briefing, I intend to provide the evidence that links him to the outstanding murders of Gemma Willis, James Wilson, and Sean McKinney.

We will start with you, please Sophie. Can you tell us what you and Chris discovered?"

Sophie approached the board and placed an overlay on it that identified a residential area. She marked the spot where CCTV had picked up a black van following its collision with a motorbike, and the spot where CCTV lost the van, which she suggested was because it had driven into the said residential area.

"We proceeded to investigate if any of the residents were known to police, and actually, we found quite a few, but one in particular had a record of violence, and that was Luke Williams, who lives here," Identifying a large plot, near the centre of the area. "The property includes a large five-bedroomed house, several outbuildings and four garages. It would be easy to store a van in any one of these. We then carried out house-to-house enquiries in our search for CCTV along these roads," Which she identified with a red marker pen. "These lead off the main drag, and we found CCTV evidence of a black van moving towards the property at the assessed time. However, the images are grainy, we cannot see the number plate or confirm that it was a Ford Custom van."

"Thank you Sophie, and I assume the property is now

under surveillance?" asked Merriman.

"Yes sir."

Fielding continued,

"This is significant information, because the black van involved in the collision, is highly likely to be the same van seen entering and leaving Darcy House. The van that we believe had Gemma's body in it, and the van responsible for the hit-and-run that killed the warden. Unfortunately, until we find the van, or have a reason to search William's property, we cannot confirm our suspicions. Jake, can we hear your report now please."

Jake stood up but kept his position. His was not a visual report, nor was it fact, but it was good circumstantial, third-party information,

"DC Fiona Wells and I are currently on assignment with the drug squad working the market. Our conversations with people confirmed that the Dog and Duck were well known as a place to buy your drug of choice, class A, B or C. The brothers who run it, Bob, and Max Welch, are fairly new to the area, having moved down from the north of England roughly two years ago. Initially, they worked for Williams helping to manage the greyhound operation, before being promoted to organising the drug runs for him. This went well for a while until the brothers decided to set up on their own. They wanted a taste of the big money, and took on the pub, already known as a place to buy soft drugs, but with their contacts, they could expand the operation into supplying hard drugs. My informant also said that Williams was incensed about it and paid the boys a visit a couple of months ago, in the middle of the night, and smashed the place up. I have checked, and there is a police report of the incident, written up as vandalism."

Merriman interrupted, "That's good information Sergeant, for the market investigation, but how does this link to the murders?"

"Sir. Because one of the brothers, Max Welch, the one responsible for sourcing and collecting the drugs, has a girlfriend, her name is Claudia Williams. Luke Williams' daughter and my informant said that she supplied Welch with Fentanyl that she stole from her father, which prompted the vandalism."

"Right. That is a good link, but the possession of Fentanyl by the brothers puts them under suspicion for the murders too, doesn't it?"

Spence spoke up, "Sir. The brothers have been under investigation by the drug squad for some months, and their surveillance confirms that they could not have been involved in Gemma Willis' murder. There is also no evidence that they ever owned or drove a black van."

Merriman seemed satisfied but wanted confirmation that the brothers would be questioned about their activities and customers, as they may well have supplied the Fentanyl used in the killings. Spence told him that all those avenues were already being investigated. Then turning back to Jake, Merriman asked,

"So, your evidence, sergeant, is just what you've heard?"

"Yes sir. Just the result of conversations, either directly with people who work on the market, or what we've overheard. The people have no idea that we're police officers."

"And I assume, as you are supposedly a market inspector, that you will be working there again today?"

"Yes sir. But not DC Wells. We feel that her presence two days in a row would create suspicion."

"Thank you." And turning to Spence, asked, "And any news from forensics on the hair found on Gemma Willis?"

"Yes sir. It has been identified as coming from a Jack

Russell breed."

"Well that is a shame, if it had been a greyhound, we'd be in a better position." Then addressing Fielding, asked, "And do you think this man Williams is the shepherd?"

"I would like to say yes. Sean McKinney told Miller that the shepherd was 'top drawer' bad. It's not a phrase I've heard used before, but apparently, it means someone of high social standing that is also a top criminal."

"Well, that sounds like Williams to me."

"What's your next move then?" asked DCS Black.

"Sir, we lost our last chance of a positive ID with the death of McKinney, so I think we'll have to go to him, to the chatroom. Flush him out that way."

"I thought we were already monitoring the chatroom?"

"Yes, we are, and as yet, the shepherd hasn't appeared. I doubt he would use that name on the chat anyway. Gemma's diary entries suggest that he requested she called him the shepherd in a private capacity. I'm suggesting we enter the chatroom, present ourselves as a desperate young girl, and attempt to engage with him."

"Do it," ordered Black. "And while we're on the subject of McKinney. Is there anything new to add to your report I received this morning?"

"Yes sir. The remainder of the squatters in the house, and the homeless camping out on the common have been booked in to be questioned today. I'm hoping we get something because so far, none have had any information that would help the enquiry. However, there is reason to suspect that the individual driving the white Mercedes, identified as having a harelip, would be a known associate of Robert Mann, owner of the vehicle. I have officers attending the prison later this morning to interview him. I will keep you updated on the outcome."

Black nodded in acknowledgement and was about to speak

when the door opened. It was a uniformed officer holding a note for Fielding.

Black was irritated by the intrusion, "Is it urgent constable?"

"Yes sir. It is."

Fielding took the note. The room was deathly quiet. The atmosphere of anticipation was almost palpable. Fielding read it and smiled.

"At last, a break!" And proceeded to read it aloud. "In the search of the tents and surrounding area on the common, a mobile phone was found. It has been confirmed as belonging to Sean McKinney!"

"Good. Let me know what you find on it."

Fielding now closed the meeting with a plea,

"We all need to make a concerted effort to find evidence of Williams' involvement in any of the crimes being investigated. I don't know if he is the shepherd, but I do know that he's a villain we need to take off the streets. Jake, do your best to find something we can use from the market. Harris and Chris, read up on everything we already know about Williams and his associates, and then do some digging. Find something that others have missed," he said. With a wink to Harris, knowing he thrived on research. "And Hearn, when you interview the homeless individuals from Putney common, focus on tracing McKinney's movements. I don't believe he came and went without anyone knowing. DI Spence and I will be interviewing Miller and his band of brothers. Don't hesitate to interrupt either of us if something breaks."

As everyone began to leave, Spence called Sophie into his office, Chris was not invited and stood looking dejected, wondering why Spence wanted to speak with her alone. He considered himself to be a good copper, competent, decisive, effective, and had never doubted his performance. That was until now, when it seemed that he was constantly side barred in favour of Sophie. She was the one they approached for her opinion, for feedback or information. Even today, it was Sophie they asked to present their findings.

In Spence's office, Sophie sat at his desk. She too was wondering why Chris wasn't included. They had become quite a double act, and she was now concerned that perhaps others had noticed that their relationship was perhaps a little too comfortable.

Spence leaned on his desk, his chin resting in the palm of his hand, "Now, Sophie." he said, in a fatherly tone.

Oh no, she thought. Here it comes, the lecture.

"Sophie, I'm not sure how I feel about this, but DCI Fielding has put you forward for the chatroom investigation."

Sophie's eyes widened. It wasn't a rollicking after all. It was an opportunity to advance herself, and she jumped at the chance of it, with no reservations,

"Yes, that's great. I'll be pleased to do it. Thank you, sir."

Spence was ordered to approach her, but he *did* have reservations. In his experience, these sorts of things have a habit of going pear-shaped, and he didn't want that for her.

"Sophie, you need to think about it. It's not going to be a bed of roses. You will be up all hours, sometimes all night just waiting and watching. You will need to take on the persona of a damaged young lady. The content you will have to digest might give you nightmares, and then you will have to converse with sadistic and perverted individuals. People that will try to get inside your head and fill it with grotesque images and negative thoughts." He had laid it on thick and was looking for a reaction.

"Yes sir, I'm aware of that." she reassured him, "I'm a strong person and ready to take it on."

Spence really wasn't comfortable, but Sophie seemed so confident and determined,

"Okay. But if you do make contact with the shepherd, you

won't be alone. Sarah will be with you, assisting you with the replies."

"Could I ask why I was put forward, sir?"

"Because you're the youngest, and more familiar with what young people think and do. And certainly more familiar with the technology and language. I also understand that you take part in amateur dramatics, which is also a bonus."

"I see. Thank you," she replied, masking her disappointment with a smile. She'd expected he would say it was because of her performance as a police officer.

"The next step then Sophie is to introduce you to our psychologist, Brenda Watson. She will provide you with information on the characteristics of poor mental health, fill you in on what to say, and how to respond. It's vital that the chatroom users, and the shepherd of course, who we believe will be observing the chatter looking for his next victim, need to believe you really are desperate and contemplating suicide."

That afternoon, having been sent home to prepare for the evening, Sophie was reading through the paperwork, and planning how she would begin her conversation in the chatroom when she heard the doorbell. Peering through the spyhole, she could see it was Chris and was in two minds about whether to open it. She was still smarting from an earlier, heated conversation, and was not in the mood for another round of it. Perhaps, she'd pretend to be out, and he would leave, but then her car was on the drive, and he'd know she was avoiding him. So, taking a deep breath, and wearing the actress' smile, she opened the door,

"Hiya! What are you doing here?"

"I need to talk to you." came the stoic reply.

She sighed, "Look. I know why you're here, and for the last time, I've said yes. I want to do it. Why can't you be pleased for me?"

"Pleased! Pleased that you're probably going to end up mentally scarred by the experience. Honestly Sophie," he pleaded, "this isn't a be-all and end-all choice. There will be other opportunities to impress."

That made her angry. She wasn't trying to impress, or so she believed, and standing with hands on hips, launched her attack,

"What gives you the right to lecture me on what I can, and can't do? Eh?"

He was biting his lip, and at first, she thought he was lost for words, but no, he was stifling a laugh, he found her stance both comical and endearing, and that made her even more angry.

"I think you'd better leave!"

"I will! I will, but I care what happens to you. Don't forget that." His attitude was open and earnest and left her in no doubt that his concern was both genuine and heartfelt.

Now she felt awful. She'd been hoping he'd notice her, and now, clearly, he did. And what's more, had shown he had feelings for her. And she'd told him to leave! Her shoulders dropped, and grasping his arm, she gave it a squeeze.

"Thank you, I will." And gently placed her cheek on his, leaving the hint of a kiss.

TEN

Friday 14th December – 21:00

Sophie arrived at the station and was shown to a purposed office for her investigation. Spence was already in attendance having overseen some of the squatter interviews and had come into her office to observe the initial entry into the chatroom. If truth be known, it was also to monitor his young up-and-coming officer. Like a father watching his child's first steps, he was full of pride, willing her on, but needed to keep her close should she need his support. Alongside him, sat Brenda Watson, the psychologist seconded into CID for as long as it takes, to advise and support her.

This wasn't originally part of the plan, but Spence put his parts on, and Fielding relented. She had already had a preparatory meeting with Sophie, where they discussed the subject of mental health and suicidal tendencies and would now be present to support her through the initial set-up. From then on, she would make herself available to speak with her whenever she felt the need, to dispel any dark thoughts and jettison the gremlins.

Another new face in attendance was Ron Hawkes, the station's IT manager. His team had been monitoring the chat for several days and was able to identify some characters to avoid, ones identified by the users as pests, or undesirables. This evening, it was his responsibility to ensure that the hardware was in good working order and be ready to address any IT failure as quickly as possible.

They all put their heads together to pick Sophie a nickname. It would appear each time she contributed to the chat, and it needed to entice the shepherd. They tried several before having one accepted. She was now Tammy16.

Ron had already opened the chatroom when Sophie sat at the PC. The conversations were scrolling on the screen, it reminded her of Twitter.

"They're going up so fast, aren't they."

Ron pulled a chair up beside her,

"The speed will depend on how many people are contributing, and that will depend on the subject matter. The more emotive, the more contributions. Now, when you join the chat, if someone is interested in what you have to say, they will respond on the main screen. If they are interested in you, they will invite you for a private chat. That will appear on a separate screen, like this," And showed her an image of the screen in his file.

"How will I know if I'm on the private screen?"

"You won't until they contact you through it. Then you will be chatting privately."

"So, at that point, I'm no longer visible on the main screen?"

"That's right. So don't waste your time chatting privately unless you suspect he is the shepherd."

"Will he not come up as the shepherd?"

At which point, they all looked at each other. She'd shown her naivety, and Spence was concerned."

"Sophie, if his name on the feed was the shepherd, we'd have caught him days ago."

Now she felt stupid. "Of course, I didn't think." And with that, had now realised how difficult this assignment was going to be. She would have to be a detective in the true sense of the word, be diligent, and look for the inference in the chat if she was going to flush him out.

Chris and Harris, who had called it a day, had signed out and were on their way to meet up with Jake for a quick drink. They'd all been on a couple of courses together, got on well and found they had a lot in common, but as yet they haven't had an occasion to work as a team.

When they arrived, Jake was sitting in the snug with three pints of beer on the table.

Chris pulled up a chair and shook Jake's hand. Harris who was in a hurry to get to the gent's, slapped him on the back as he passed by.

Chris untied his scarf and slumped down. "What a bloody day."

"Why? What's up mate?"

Chris seemed to squirm, he didn't really want to say, but it was too late, his opening comment meant he needed to provide an answer.

"It's Sophie."

"What about her? Stealing the limelight again, is she? he asked flippantly.

"Worse. Much worse, she's put herself in danger."

"How come?"

Chris explained that Sophie had agreed to take on the chatroom assignment and that he didn't feel she was experienced enough or streetwise enough to do it. He'd convinced himself that she would be harmed in some way.

Jake dismissed his concerns, "No way would they let her be exposed to danger. Not if the DI is involved. He's a right worryguts, especially with the females."

"Yeah, that's what Harris thinks too, but I'm not sure." To him, something didn't feel right.

Harris had now returned, and practically downed half his pint in one gulp.

"Thirsty, are we?" laughed Jake.

Harris wiped the froth off his mouth with the back of his hand, "Too right. It's thirsty work all this research. Anyway, how is it at the exciting end?"

"Truthfully, a bit slow."

"It didn't sound it in the briefing. You had loads to report in just one day on the job."

Jake tapped his nose, "Between you and me, it wasn't that hard. It's all about who you choose to talk to, and my informant was a girl I dated last year."

Harris looked alarmed, "She knows you're a copper?"

"Yep. But she won't tell."

"How can you be so sure?"

Jake winked, "Because she knows I'll tell her husband what we got up to if she did."

A shake of the head, and an awkward smile, expressed what Chris thought of it. And Harris? Well, he just continued to look alarmed.

Jake elbowed him in the arm, "It's fine Harris. Chill. The only problem now is that she's told me all she knows, and nobody else is talking. I reckon you'd have to work on that bloody market for years before anyone would trust you."

"So, what's the plan?" asked Chris.

"I've got one more day, and I'm on camera duty snapping the punters. Hopefully, something will come of it."

"Oh, that sounds boring," said Harris, "You'll need a drink after that one."

"Too bloody right," agreed Jake. Downing the final dregs of his pint before making his apologies and leaving. Apparently, he had another date waiting for his attention.

Back in the chatroom, Sophie had joined in with the chat on euthanasia. Ron had instructed her to offer small comments to begin with so her nickname would be popping up regularly. She complied but hoped that just tapping out 'I agree' or 'no way' would only be a short-term measure. She was ready and eager to get involved.

Spence had now left the room and was in a meeting with Merriman and Fielding.

"How's it progressing?" asked Merriman.

"All seems fine. She's logged in and engaged with the chat."

"I suppose it's an unknown as to when the shepherd approaches her, or if he does, come to that."

"Yes sir. Let's hope we're lucky, God knows we deserve some luck."

"I agree, but it's not going our way at the moment. We tried for a search warrant for Williams' premises and cars on what we had but was refused on the grounds of insufficient evidence."

Spence was relieved. He really wasn't sure that Williams was their man for the murders anyway. In his opinion, there was absolutely no doubt that he was a thug and a villain. A man who wouldn't blink an eye at doing away with someone in his business that had let him down, crossed him or whom he didn't trust. But murdering a young girl with a fatal dose of Fentanyl? Why? It didn't sit well with him. And as for a hit-and-run that wasn't his style either.

"What about McKinney's mobile? Is there nothing on that of any use?"

Fielding shook his head, "There's nothing to identify that it was Williams he was texting, and if he was in contact with him, then he must have been using a pay-as-you-go. None of Williams' known numbers appear. But it will help us to identify McKinney's last movements." Fielding sighed in frustration. "If only we could find some sound evidence."

Merriman picked his coat off the stand and walked towards the door, signalling with his hand that he expected them to do the same, "I think what we all need to find, is our beds. After a good night's sleep, we'll all be refreshed and can resume the hunt tomorrow. Go get one, and I'll see you both in the morning."

In the chatroom, Sophie was feeling confident and comfortable. She'd come across one of the undesirables identified by Ron and declined the invitation to chat privately. They responded by giving the finger. Not the shepherd's style at all, she thought. If he is a professional, he would have a bit of class and decided to focus on the more educated and succinct responses.

There was one in particular that, like her, had been on the chat for several hours. Their nickname, London4136 giving nothing away as to their gender or age, which she expected is what the shepherd would choose. Would she be so lucky to get his attention on the first try? She doubted it, but it intrigued her, and boldly invited them into a private chat. A few moments later, it was accepted, and now the butterflies in her stomach began.

Tammy16	*You've been online, like me, for a long time tonight.*
London4136	*I'm always on for a long time.*
Tammy16	*Why?*
London4136	*Nothing else to do.*
Tammy16	*What? No hobbies?*
London4136	*Hobbies are few and far between when you have no legs.*
Tammy16	*Oh. Sorry. I didn't mean to upset you.*
London4136	*You didn't. I'm fine with it now. Bloody Diabetes, but it just gets lonely sometimes.*
Tammy16	*I bet it does.*
London4136	*Why are you wasting your time here?*
Tammy 16	*I guess I'm lonely too.*
London4136	*Are you disabled like me?*

Tammy16	*In a way.*
London4136	*What way? Come on. I opened up to you.*
Tammy16	*I find it hard to make friends and needed someone to talk to.*
London4136	*Everyone on here feels the same way, but be careful, there are some right weirdos about. I'm off now. It's bedtime for me. Keep safe and speak again sometime.*

The abrupt end was unexpected and left her confused. If it was the shepherd, he'd want to keep chatting wouldn't he? Or perhaps that's how he starts off, leaving you feeling that you're not that important. It certainly was puzzling, but now the conversation had ended, just like London4136, she too was ready to put her head down on a soft pillow. Disappointed with nothing to report, reluctantly, she handed over to an IT technician, one of the team who would be monitoring the chatroom while she was away.

"Tomorrow's another day," he proclaimed. As she pulled on her coat.

She smiled, "Yes. Yes, it is, isn't it."

Eleven

Saturday 15th December – 05:30

Jake had walked onto the market just as the traders were setting up. It was still dark, and following his encounter with a frisky, and over-amorous barmaid, he'd had barely any sleep, and sported unshaven stubble, that in no way could be considered designer. This was not the appearance he wanted to give, but ironically, now that he looked unkempt, the traders seemed to respond better towards him, more like one of them, and less like a stuck-up official.

Of course, he would take advantage of it. Firstly by accepting a bacon butty off the catering van, and secondly, enjoying a 'hair of the dog' with the pensioner watchmaker. How he managed, being three sheets to the wind most of the day, to successfully navigate the intricacies of a watch movement, nobody knew.

Considering the best place to base himself, he decided on Joe's café, which sat nestled between the tailor and the off-licence. His decision was based on information received from the team leader, confirming drug dealing was taking place in the recreation ground. Therefore, the café being opposite, would be an ideal position to watch all the coming and going, especially as it was a Saturday. The day when regular traders are joined by car booters. Their stalls began near the Dog and Duck pub, and depending on the number could occupy every inch of the recreation ground boundary.

He sat in the main window to the side of a large-leafed plant, joking with the waitress that he'd bagged the best table, beside the radiator. This was partly the case; the temperature outside still hadn't risen above freezing yet. But in truth, the position of the plant would enable him to snap away on his phone without it being too obvious to the other customers, and what's more, the waitress had agreed to save the table for him while he carried out his walkabouts. His charm with the ladies working its magic again.

His drug squad colleagues had now arrived, and as they passed the café, acknowledged his presence with a scratch of their nose. Jake was being kept up to date on the plan to move the operation to the car boot section and was very much aware of the important part he would play. With no CCTV coverage of the recreation ground, everyone would be banking on his pictures to produce something of interest. He was instructed to text the images directly to the drug squad office, where they would be checked against their records, and anyone identified as having form for drug offences would be flagged for surveillance.

With everyone in place, the operation was underway. Jake had been given guidance on what to look out for in an individual, after all, the last thing anyone wanted was a host of random images. Each one would have to be the result of a considered decision based on the individual's demeanour, Do they appear edgy, interested in what's happening around them, as if on the lookout? Are they hanging about or returning to the same spot? Do they seem to have short interactions with others? And are they carrying a backpack in their arms? This was considered to be the essential kit for a dealer as if approached by the police, they could ditch it – the last thing they want is to be caught with drugs on their person.

Unfortunately, many people carry a backpack, and many people will have characteristics similar to his guidance. So, at the end of the day, it really came down to his copper's nose, and whether or not he thought they were acting suspiciously.

As it turned out, his intuition was reaping rewards. In the

second half of the morning, he identified a dealer. They kept him under surveillance for two hours, recording his interactions before making an arrest, and as a result, ten buyers were followed, apprehended, and charged with possession.

Being pleased with his performance and success, it could have been that he became too relaxed, or over-confident. Whatever it was, he'd caught the eye of a car booter. A man who'd obviously had time on his hands to watch what was going on around him and believing Jake to be a pervert taking pictures of children, dialled nine-nine-nine. Within minutes, two burly officers had him by the arm, confiscated his phone, and patted him down in full view of everybody. Jake had no option but to be compliant, he couldn't produce his police ID which was back at the station, and he was undercover anyway. Once in the back of the squad car, he was able to confirm who he was, but it was too late, his part in the day was over.

Back at the station, he was sat at his desk downloading the images from his phone onto a PC, when Harris and Chris walked in.

"You're back earlier than expected," observed Harris.

Jake made no reply, just threw him a look that clearly identified he was in a bad place, and to approach with caution. Chris grabbed Harris by the sleeve and was about to pull him away when he noticed the images scrolling on the PC.

"Which ones are dealers?" asked Chris. Not too bothered if he upset him, he was bigger and stronger anyway, and Jake knew it.

He pointed to a male on the far right of the screen. Harris also looked, "I don't know him, but I do know that one."

Jake looked up, "Which one?"

"That woman at the bottom on the left."

Jake enlarged the image to fit the screen, "She's one of the buyers that got a first offence warning notice. How do you know her?"

"That, my friends, is Sammi Mancini."

Twelve

Sunday 16th December – 19:30

The alarm had been set to snooze on at least two occasions, and once more would leave Sophie little or no time to get prepared for work. This she knew, but the long nights watching the screen, in a poorly lit room with no success was taking its toll, and today she struggled to get motivated. She had expected the assignment to be exciting, it was after all, an undercover operation, she was the cuckoo in the nest, but it had turned out to be dull and boring.

She hadn't been affected too much by the chatter and therefore had only found the need to speak to Brenda Watson on a couple of occasions. But she did feel sorry for some of the poor souls with no life away from the chatroom, and empathy for those who told of their desperation. What she was hoping to feel was that rush of adrenaline when the shepherd made an appearance, and the prospect of that wasn't looking likely. As she showered, the tepid water aided her recovery from the comatose effect. Her thoughts were lucid once more, and she started to recall and think about her recent experience online.

She had been following a chat on the merits of over-the-counter well-being remedies, and for once it was interesting. She was an exponent of good well-being, and in her opinion, anything that promotes the feeling of wellness should be considered. Everyone seemed to be on the same page with it, so to speak, until Abram122 cropped up with crass remarks, then irritated everybody with his forthright opinions. Berating anyone who chose to share their experience with home remedies, calling them dangerous and charlatans. Consequently, many of them stopped contributing, and in the end, it was like a bunfight between two opposing sides. Sophie didn't have the luxury of a choice to leave the chat, she had to sit and watch the drivel being spewed out. It made her angry, and she hoped he wouldn't be rearing his head again today.

When she arrived at her office, it seemed like a delegation was waiting for her. Spence stood behind the desk resting his arm on the top of the PC, while Sarah stood leaning against the filing cabinet. Ron Hawkes was sitting at the desk watching the chatter scroll up, and Brenda Watson sat in the corner, holding a clipboard, and looking very serious.

Sophie's expression was one of surprise. "Is everything okay?"

Spence ushered her to a chair beside Ron, "Your feed last night was reviewed, and it seems that a good deal of it was taken up by a contributor called Abram122."

"Oh him. He made the night very long."

"I'm sure. Ron has shown us some of the unpleasant rhetoric."

He pulled up another chair, and sat beside her, "Ron also made the connection between Abram122 and the shepherd."

"What?" she exclaimed, "How?"

As it turned out, Ron was a religious man, and knew that Abram, later known as Abraham, was considered a shepherd in the Bible, God's chosen one, and the 122, Ron suggested may refer to Genesis 12.2. Spence read it out,

"I will make your name great, and you will be a blessing."

At which point they all looked to Brenda for her professional comment. She turned and addressed Spence directly, "I'm not a criminal psychologist, but I would imagine he believes that he is the chosen one."

The look on Spence's face conveyed his disappointment. He guessed that for himself and he was now thinking that perhaps he needed to find a criminal psychologist instead.

Sophie on the other hand felt empty. She'd failed and was expecting to be relieved of her duties, but no, that wasn't the plan at all. They had already decided amongst themselves that changing the person contributing to the chat would be noticeable. Sophie had a certain way with words, and the concern was that Abram122 might notice a change that would send him back into the dark. They needed to keep him in the light of the chatroom, and hopefully to entice him into a private chat.

Sophie was concerned, "What should I say in the chat?" Worried that her lack of experience would ruin their chances of catching him.

Spence put a hand on her shoulder, "You can use your own words, but Sarah will be guiding you on how to respond to build a relationship with him."

Sophie understood what was needed to do to trap this monster, but it didn't stop her body from reacting to the thought of it by producing a tremble in her knees, and butterflies in her stomach. She must have looked scared because it prompted Sarah to put an arm around her, and give her a squeeze,

"We'll catch the bastard together," she whispered.

Spence then left them all to discuss how to proceed. He was needed in the main office to hear the feedback from the day's investigations into Sammi Mancini.

The CID office had been buzzing when they heard the news that she was caught buying class B drugs in the market. This was particularly significant because it could suggest a link to the weed being supplied to the Darcy residents, and as far as Spence was concerned, it may be her first offence on paper, but that only confirms it was the first time she'd been caught.

He couldn't believe that she came across a dealer by

accident and made an ill-judged decision to buy from him. He was convinced that she knew the dealer would be there and went prepared to buy. Which also implied that she knew him, and almost definitely had bought from him before. The next step was therefore to order a background check, and he felt sure that it would unearth some skeletons.

Throughout the day, the team had been hard at it, and ironically it was the lack of skeletons that was most revealing. It didn't matter which avenue they investigated, nobody could find any information on her, prior to two thousand and ten. It seems she just appeared on the radar in June of that year when she took up a junior position with the council. Clearly, they hadn't carried out their due diligence before taking her on.

Spence remembered it being the year of both a general election and local elections. At a time when local agencies were suffering from staff shortages and budget cuts, and with all the disruption, he wouldn't have been surprised if the administration department hadn't taken the biggest hit.

It was now that Spence remembered her telling him when they first met at Darcy House following Gemma's murder, that she'd just returned from a course in Scotland. He now needed to know if this was in fact the case. He could have just called Social Services to confirm it, but then she would get to hear of it and know she was under investigation. This had to be avoided at all costs until he was satisfied that she had no part in Gemma's, or the other's deaths.

So who was she? They were now tasked with the job of digging into her past, without raising any flags, and the best person to head up that team would be DS Jake Madden. Which is how it was written in Spence's report to Fielding requesting resources.

Jake chose Chris Sparkes, Peter Hearn, and Harris to make up the dream team. The next stage was to decide on a plan of action.

"Firstly, I think we should identify exactly when our subject was first recorded as being Sammi Mancini. We can't just assume it was when she started work at the council. She may have been in London or elsewhere in the country long before that."

"Absolutely," agreed Harris. "And if she has changed her identity, what would be the first thing anyone would need to do?"

"Perhaps registering with a doctor or getting a driving license?" suggested Chris.

Hearn thought that unlikely, "You'd need ID for both of those though, and for the driving license, you'd also have to take a test or prove you've held a license before."

"So, it seems to me that she either took on somebody else's identity, bought forged documents, or moved here from abroad?" He quite liked the last option, "That could be a possibility, couldn't it?" concluded Jake.

It was therefore agreed that Chris and Peter would check with DVLA and the passport office, to see if she had made any applications, and if so, to identify who were her referees. They would also check with MISPERS for any female, similar age, and build, missing with the name Mancini or similar. Jake and Harris would check with Immigration for any female the same age entering the country.

Spence was now about to hear their news. Jake asked Chris to report first,

"Following our enquiries with missing persons, we can confirm that there is no record of a female her age or similar reported missing, in either the first part of two thousand and ten or for the year two thousand and nine. With regards to DVLA and the Passport office, they say that any documents she holds must be forgeries, as they have no record of her applying for either."

"Well, knowing that nothing sinister is associated with her new identity is a relief anyway. Good work."

Jake, then asked Harris to relay what they had found out.

"We checked the immigration records, and nobody was identified as Mancini, however, in February of that year, they do have a record of a female entering the country on a work visa from Ireland, aged eighteen."

"That's only a couple of years adrift." interrupted Spence.

"Sir. And her name is Samantha Mann. We have tried to trace her whereabouts, but the address she gave on her entry was false."

"This is sounding very promising, very promising indeed. Do we have a picture of this Samantha Mann?"

Jake pulled up a photo on his laptop," This is what we received from Immigration, it's the photo on her Irish passport."

Together, they checked it against the image Jake took at the market. To and fro, from one to the other, they scrutinised and discussed the features. And after a long session involving the rubbing of chins, and shaking of heads, the ID was inconclusive.

"She looks young. When was the Irish photo taken?" asked Spence.

"The passport expired in December, two thousand and ten. So her photo would have been taken five years before that."

"It's no bloody wonder we're struggling then, that photo was taken fifteen years ago. She's only thirteen in this one!" Pointing to the Irish passport.

"Jake, get the boys in forensics to map the face. If it's her, they'll be able to confirm it. But hang on, if her passport expired in two thousand and ten, that also means that she hasn't renewed her Irish passport, doesn't it? Why?"

"Because she's in England sir?"

"Could be."

"Yes, sir. And I'm sure that name, Mann, rings a bell. Does it with anyone else?"

"I thought so too." agreed Chris, "but I can't think where I've heard it."

"I know exactly where." chirped Harris. "It's the same name as the white Mercedes owner, Robert Mann."

Back in the chatroom office, Sophie had logged in and was watching the chat, along with Sarah who had just returned with some welcome tea and biscuits.

"Poor you, I don't think I could stomach two full shifts watching this. It's awful."

Sophie agreed, "I know. You can't believe people really have these thoughts, can you? Last night, one person was trying to convince everyone that aliens had moved into her shed!"

Sarah laughed out loud, "After what I've just read, I think she might be right!"

Both officers enjoying having a giggle as they shared out the bourbon biscuits. Sophie, in particular was enjoying the company and conversation. Since joining the force, she hadn't had the time or the opportunity to make friends and missed the girly nights of her teens.

Her plate now empty and wellbeing topped up, she asked,

"Shall I start to contribute something now?"

"Absolutely. I can't stand much more of this! No wonder Abram's gone AWOL."

Sophie laughed. She appreciated the humour, but it hadn't helped the way she felt. That first contribution to the chat always made her tense. She couldn't explain why, but now her shoulders were taught and rigid, her mouth dry, and for the third time in an hour, she needed a pee.

"Sorry Sophie, you're going to have to hold it in. Look."

And there he was, Abram122.

Sophie felt the adrenaline rising, "What shall we write?"

"That depends. What's he contributing to?"

"The chat appears to have developed into a discussion on whether or not to include 'obey' in the marriage vows."

"What's his opinion?"

Sophie pointed to his last comment.

"Oh he's definitely sitting on the fence saying it's a personal choice, isn't he. What we need to do Sophie, is to write something emotive. Something to get him interested in Tammy16."

Sophie agreed but was lost for ideas.

"Okay. Let's think about this. If he is the shepherd, he will be on the lookout for someone vulnerable, someone he can manipulate. Perhaps someone who is lonely."

"I tried that with London4136, and it didn't get any response. They told me everyone on the chat was lonely."

"Right. What about presenting Tammy16 as a young girl needing help and advice?"

That suggestion prompted a moment of thought, ultimately broken by Sarah, who intimated with her hands for Sophie to start typing.

Tammy16 *Does anyone know of a homeless shelter for girls in south London?*

London4136 *Oh Tammy. Has it come to that?*

Tammy16 *I need a place to go.*

London4136 *Think before you act and be careful who you accept help from.*

Monty666 *Shut up London, you always think the worst of people.*

London4136 *I'm just telling her how it is, there are weirdos on here.*

Monty666 *And you're not?*

London4136 *What d'you mean?*

"Oh goodness," grumbled Sophie, "this isn't going to be

easy, is it? They've gone off on each other, and Tammy16 has been lost in the fray!"

Sarah was also frustrated and suggested that they needed to keep contributing, rather than waiting for a response, then at least, the name would keep appearing.

Tammy16 *I didn't mean to cause a fight. I just wanted some advice.*
Sheila3232 *Try Google.*
London4136 *Oh that's helpful. Not.*
Tammy16 *I need to leave this place.*
Abram122 *You sound too young to be out on your own.*

There was a sharp intake of breath. Sophie was excited, "Quick! What should we write?"

"He wants to know your age, if you are sixteen or not."

Tammy16 *That's what my carers say, but they're wrong.*
London4136 *Carers? Girl, get off this chat. It's no place for you.*
Sheila3232 *Leave the girl alone, stop with the morality police shit.*
Abram122 *Take no notice London, you're doing a good job.*
London4136 *Thanks Abram.*
Abram122 *You're welcome.*
Tammy16 *Thank you too London, and you Abram.*

They continued contributing for some time, waiting for Abram to return, but as time ticked away, it became less and less likely. Eventually, the message came up, Abram122 has left the chat.

Sophie griped, "We've lost him."

Sarah however, thought it was interesting that although he hadn't been contributing, he must have been watching the exchanges, and her instinct was that he would be intrigued by Tammy16's predicament. She was right, and they didn't have to wait long, within the hour a message came through that Abram122 wanted a private chat.

Sarah called Spence. "He's taken the bait."

"On my way."

Sophie was now concerned about the delay in replying, but Sarah said that he would expect a delay. He wouldn't know what Tammy16 was doing at the time. She could easily be away from her device and felt sure that they would make contact before he gave up waiting. Within minutes, Spence blasted into the room,

"What's happening?"

"Sophie is about to accept his invitation and chat with him privately."

"Great. Go for it, Sophie. Let's catch ourselves a shepherd."

Abram122	*I saw you on the chat yesterday, and you were like a little mouse.*
Tammy16	*What do you mean?*
Abram122	*I was watching. You were timid.*
Tammy16	*I'm new and I was nervous.*
Abram122	*Are you nervous about everything?*
Tammy16	*Only if it's scary.*
Abram122	*What scares you little one?*

"He's trying to get inside your head?" said Spence. "Make sure he knows that you're vulnerable."

Tammy16	*Being on my own.*
Abram122	*Are you on your own now?*
Tammy16	*Yes. In this awful place.*

Abram122	*Where are you? And why are you there sweetheart?"*

"There it is!" cried Spence, "That's how he referred to Gemma, as sweetheart."

"He's befriending her, making her feel special," said Sarah.

Tammy16	*It's a long story.*
Abram122	*And what about your family? Why aren't you with them?*

"Tell him you don't have one," instructed Spence.

Tammy16	*I don't have a family.*
Abram122	*Everyone has a family of some sort. Someone who cares about you. Where are yours?*
Tammy16	*Do I have to say?*
Abram122	*Not if you don't want to. But I'd like to help you. Do you have any friends?*
Tammy16	*No.*
Abram122	*Oh I can't believe that you don't have friends, a teenager always has friends.*
Tammy16	*I don't. The others here are all weird.*
Abram122	*Here? Where's here?*
Tammy16	*I don't want to say.*
Abram122	*I understand. Are you able to leave?*

"I expect he's already guessed you're in a home, but now he's checking it's not a youth offender's facility," said Sarah.

Tammy16	*Yes.*
Abram122	*That's good. You can get out and make friends. Have you tried joining a youth club?*
Tammy16	*No. I don't make friends easily.*

Abram122 *Do you like dogs?*

All three looked at each other – what was coming next?

Tammy16 *Yes, I do, but I can't have one.*
Abram122 *That's a shame. Dogs make excellent friends.*
Tammy16 *Perhaps one day.*
Abram122 *Perhaps. Until then I will be your friend.*
Tammy16 *Thank you.*
Abram122 *I have to go now. Work to do. Keep safe sweetheart. Speak again soon.*

They all watched and waited, it seemed ages, but it was only a minute until the message came that he'd left the chat. Everyone seemed to relax and exhale as if they'd all been holding their breath.

Sophie was concerned, "That was an abrupt ending, wasn't it. Do you think he's suspicious?"

Sarah shook her head, "I can't see why. You held back on your family, and where you were living. I think we got the balance right."

So, what do we all think?" asked Spence. "Is he our man?"

"It's too early to say, isn't it." replied Sarah. "What do you think Sophie."

"Putting myself in Tammy's shoes, I think he sounds nice, and I would want to speak with him again, so he could be."

"Okay then. We move forward with him as the prime suspect, but I also want you to scrutinise everyone who joins in with the chat, just in case.

THIRTEEN

Monday 17th December

Despite having only a few hours of sleep, Spence had been at his desk by seven o'clock as usual. Technically, he was on the day shift all week, but being on call to oversee the chatroom, had required him to be close at hand, and that meant securing a bed in the section house a few minutes away. Convenient it may have been, restful it certainly wasn't, with officers coming and going at all times throughout the night, and not one of them knowing how to close a door without slamming it.

The day played out much as he had planned. Firstly he attended Miller's appearance at the magistrates' court, and as expected he was remanded. However, Miller unable to let an opportunity to rant against the establishment go by, protested against his incarceration on the grounds that he was a free spirit, and not subject to the law or decisions of the court. Needless to say, his tirade was ignored.

On Spence's return, he made a B-line for the canteen and one of Rosie's all-day breakfasts, before finishing the morning on a mixture of reports, meetings, and paperwork.

He learned that Robert Mann was an Irishman and that he did indeed have a sister. Efforts were now underway to investigate if she was the right age, and whether or not she was still living in Ireland. If Mancini is his sister, it would be reasonable to suspect that she also knew the Mercedes driver and should all these connections prove to be the case, then Ms Mancini must be considered a suspect in Gemma's murder.

In the afternoon, he'd received a call from social services to say that Jasmine Wright was given the all-clear by the doctor and was now able to attend an interview. This could provide a breakthrough in the case. He would request that Sammi Mancini accompanied Jasmine to act as appropriate adult, giving him the opportunity, to not only quiz Jasmine about who was coming and going at Darcy house, but also to probe Mancini for information.

The interview was scheduled for the following day at nine o'clock in the morning, mainly because Fielding wanted to be present. He saw it as an opportunity to offer up some photos of individuals, one being Williams, in the hope that Jasmine would recognise him as a Darcy house visitor. His efforts with the other residents had proved unsuccessful, but as Jasmine was a close friend of Gemma, she may know more. At the end of the day, this confirmation would be enough to secure a search warrant.

In the meantime, and not one to bank on anything, he was making a visit to Donald Fallows in prison. He'd heard that the man was having a bad time of it and was going to use all his powers of persuasion, and influence with the authorities, to convince him to roll on Williams. Spence thought the price to achieve it would be too high to pay for both Fallows, and the authorities, but wished him luck as he left.

Sophie had now arrived at the station for her session in the chatroom. As she parked up, Jake was approaching his car, that was parked in the bay opposite. He waited for her to get out and walked over. His swagger had now come into play, his chest seemed to puff out, and running a hand through his hair, asked, "How's it going Sophie? Are you coping?" His manner, if intended to show concern, or more likely, intended as a pretext to start chatting her up, came across as very patronizing.

Now, Sophie could be naive at times, but not when it came to men, especially Jake's type. Being the only girl in a family of six children, she was well used to dealing with males and their many faults and had learned to shake off a negative comment and move on. However, the comment, are you coping? Inferring that she was a weak woman taking on a man's job, could not be overlooked.

"Coping with what Jake?" she asked brusquely. "The weather? Yes, it's cold and icy, but I'm wrapped up. The car? Yes, it's a bit of a banger but she's running well. Or. Am I coping with an arrogant copper, who should know better?"

For once, Jake was lost for words. His expression was that of a man who'd just been brought down to size. He raised both hands as if in surrender and walked away. She too walked off muttering to herself. Had she gone too far, he was a sergeant after all. But he was off duty, so convinced herself that it didn't matter. What did matter, was the fact he said it at all, and that got her wondering if all the men at the station felt the same way about women officers. She certainly had her doubts about Chris. He was always checking up on her, making sure she was okay, and offering to take over. Perhaps they did perceive women as less capable, but then they had a woman in the highest of police roles, or would they view that as an exception?

By the time Sophie arrived at her room, she was in a warrior mindset. It was her ambition now to prove that women officers stood shoulder to shoulder with the men, and she would start her campaign by succeeding in her mission to trap and apprehend the shepherd.

Sarah was already ensconced in her seat with a hot cup of tea in one hand and a bacon roll in the other. Knowing her to be an advocate of healthy eating, Sophie was surprised to see her munching on fast food.

"I know, I know, but it's my hormones playing up again. I just need to eat some rubbish. Can't explain it, I just have to do it." Leaning into her bag, she pulled out a couple of chocolate bars, and placing one in front of Sophie, pleaded,

"Don't make me eat them both."

Sophie was happy to oblige, being one of those people we all love to hate, can eat anything, and still keeps her figure.

Ron was now ready to pass control of the chatroom over to Sophie and Sarah. His team had been monitoring the chat since their last session and he wanted to feed back first.

"This is a record of the activity that you will want to know about." Identifying the contributors in terms of percentage of time online. "As you can see, Abram122 has not appeared at all, and checking back over the last few days, he only makes an appearance after six o'clock. However, London4136 has spent a high percentage of the day on the chat, in fact, almost sixty per cent."

Spence had walked in midway and wanted to know what it all meant.

Ron wasn't too sure himself, except he felt confident in saying London4136 most likely didn't have a job, and Abram122 did. And by following the chat, they had gleaned London4136 to be around thirty years of age, very distrusting of people, and doubted they had a disability.

"But they told me, they didn't have any legs," remarked Sophie.

"Yes, I know. But they've given themselves away several times by mentioning what they had been doing. On one chat, they said they'd been a competitor in the London marathon."

"You can do that Ron, in a wheelchair," stated Sarah.

"Yes, you can," agreed Ron. "But as one half of a horse?"

"Oh!" giggled Sophie. "They've made a mistake there. God, you can't trust anyone, can you?"

"Not in a chatroom Sophie. No." replied Ron.

"So that puts London4136 back in the frame then, doesn't it." declared Sarah.

"Yep, it's going to be an interesting night," said Spence.

Sophie was still giggling when she joined the chat. They

were discussing if vampires really exist. Monty666 was keeping it light-hearted with flippant comments, and all seemed to be enjoying it. That was until London4136 contributed.

London4136	*When you're alone, and the nights are long, even a visit from a vampire would be good.*
Monty666	*Has anyone got a violin?*
Sheila3232	*Don't be mean Monty. What's up luv?*
Cambridge99	*?*
Roddy1212	*?*

"What is London up to I wonder?" asked Sophie.

"No idea, but she's certainly creating suspense and interest."

"Sarah, d'you think London's a woman?"

"Yes, don't you?"

"What made you think that?"

"It's just her manner, I suppose."

London4136	*My cat hasn't come home.*
Sheila3232	*Ahh. Do you think it's come to harm?*
Cambridge99	*Nah. Cats stray all the time.*
Monty666	*And when did this happen? You've never mentioned a cat before.*

"Oh Sarah, I don't think he likes London at all. He's never got a good word to say to her."

"You're right. He doesn't sound very nice, does he."

Spence was standing behind them listening to their conversation,

"Be careful ladies, you're starting to assume they're male or female, and that's dangerous. We don't know who they are. Could all be con artists, for all we know."

The pair agreed. But there it was again. He called them

ladies. They weren't ladies, they were officers, and it sent Sophie's blood boiling.

"I'd like to get started now. We're wasting time chatting."

Sarah noticing Sophie's change in mood but not in tune with the reason why,

"Yep. Let's get going."

Tammy16	*Cats are nice to own but they're not loyal, are they?*
Monty666	*I was wondering where you were. Just got back from work, have you?*

Sophie turned to Sarah, "Where have I been?"

"What about shopping?"

Tammy16	*No. I've been out at the shops all day.*
Monty666	*Must have loads of dosh then.*
Tammy16	*Just my weekly allowance.*
London4136	*Don't give too much away Tammy.*
Monty666	*Here we go. Shut your face London.*
Abram122	*I think we've all heard enough from you Monty.*

"Here he is!" called Sophie. And Spence came running in.

"What's going on now?"

"Not much, he's just joined."

Monty666	*Oh another part-timer. We're not good enough to talk to during the day, are we, Abram?*
Abram122	*Some of us need to work Monty.*
Monty666	*Poor you. Some of us don't.*
London4136	*Benefits only go so far Monty.*
Monty666	*Talk for yourself, I'm not a scrounger.*
London4136	*Sounds like I've hit a nerve.*

Monty666 *Sounds to me like you've been hitting the juice, again.*
London4136 has left the chat.

Sarah sighed, "It seems like she's not up for a fight tonight, or perhaps, she has lost her cat?"
"Could be. Abram's very quiet isn't he."
"Let's draw him into a private chat again."

Tammy16 *Why are people so mean to each other on here?*
Sheila3232 *Because they've got nothing better to do.*
Abram122 *We're not all mean Tammy. You have to choose your friends carefully.*
Monty666 *Here we go again, another hero.*
Abram122 has left the chat.

"Oh, bloody hell. That Monty has chased Abram away now!"
"I doubt it Sophie. In fact, I'd go as far as to say, that if he did, then Abram is not our man."
Abram122 has joined the chat.
"He's back."
"But he's not contributing. Just watching," observed Spence.
"That's because he wants a private chat. Look," Sophie pointed to a pop-up on the screen.
Spence had now pulled up a chair and sat beside them, "Here we go!"

Abram122 *Good evening, little one.*
Tammy16 *Hi Abram.*
Abram122 *I apologise for the poor behaviour of some in the chatroom.*
Tammy16 *That's okay. It's not your fault.*

Abram122	*It's disappointing when all you want is a friendly chat, and then it gets ugly.*
Tammy16	*Yes. Monty doesn't seem to like anyone.*
Abram122	*Don't even mention his name. He's a horrible person and should be banned.*
Tammy16	*Why don't they ban him?*
Abram122	*I guess because they know he's a lonely soul like the rest of us.*

"Ask him if he's lonely," ordered Spence.

Tammy16	*Are you lonely Abram?*
Abram122	*Sometimes Tammy. It would be nice to have a friend close by sometimes.*

"Close by? Question that Sophie."

Tammy16	*Do all your friends live a long way away?*
Abram122	*Yes. In the north of England. I don't see them much.*

"What part of the north? Nail it down."

Tammy16	*I've never been north. What's it like?*
Abram122	*Colder! Ha Ha.*
Tammy16	*Oh. So is it near Scotland?*
Abram122	*It's a decent drive from here. Hopefully, you will travel more when you're older.*

"He's not going to give it up, is he."

Tammy16	*Yes. I hope so too.*
Abram122	*I've got some brilliant pictures of the place. Would you like to see them?*

"And how's he going to do that I wonder. Ask him how Sophie."

Tammy16	*I would like to see them. How can I see them?*
Abram122	*What devices do you have? Computer, laptop, or tablet?*

"What shall I say I have? Don't forget I'm thirteen and in a children's home."

"Jasmine isn't much older, and she had a tablet, an iPad I think," said Sarah.

Tammy16	*I have an iPad.*
Abram122	*Great. I can't send them because mine doesn't work for some reason. But I could Facetime you and show them to you that way.*

"He's wanting to make face-to-face contact. This would be how he starts, and then encourages them to expose themselves."

Sophie looked alarmed but Spence reassured her that she will not be required to go that far. They would have to keep him on a string until they can trace where he is.

Tammy16	*I don't think my carer would let me do that.*
Abram122	*That's not a problem – we won't tell her. It will be our little secret. Just a couple of mates meeting up online. You won't get into trouble.*
Tammy16	*I don't know you.*
Abram122	*You'll never know me if we don't meet. I'm harmless, I just want to be your friend. I think you need one. Your life sounds like the pits.*

"I think he's trying to sound like a young person, the

language has changed," observed Sarah.

Tammy16	*I need to think about it.*
Abram122	*I understand. It would be good if we can meet. I think you need a friend, and I'm a good, caring friend. Think of me as a Shepherd, caring for all the little lost lambs.*

"Bingo! It's him," shouted Spence. Just as Fielding and Brenda Watson entered the room.

"He wants a face-to-face with Sophie."

Brenda moved in closer to look at the screen. She was reading the exchange.

"What do you think we should do?" asked Fielding.

"Say no. It's too early. He will suspect something. Trust me, I've had experience with these sorts of people, and he will be expecting to invest much more time and effort into snaring her. You will lose him if she capitulates now."

Spence and Fielding were in a dilemma. Although Brenda was the professional, and she seemed very confident in her opinion, the worry was that Abram might lose interest in Tammy16, and then he would be lost to them. The time was ticking by, and Sophie was getting anxious,

"I need to reply, sir."

Yes, she did, and both men knew they couldn't procrastinate any longer,

"Okay Sophie, just end it for the night," ordered Fielding. "And let's hope we've done the right thing."

Tammy16	*I need to go now, but I will think about it. Goodnight.*

And logged off the chat.

Stressed and exhausted, Sophie relaxed into her chair. The

pressure was off. The others were a mixture of elated by the result and bewildered by the exchanges. Fielding turned to Brenda,

"What would you suggest we do next?"

"It's important that Tammy16 doesn't succumb to his requests immediately. She appears both naïve and vulnerable, qualities that he looks for in a victim, and she certainly has something worth chasing."

"Which is?"

"Her innocence. But at this stage, he will still be unsure of her. He will need more convincing before he actually attempts the face-to-face."

With the chatroom handed over to the monitors, Sarah signed out, and Sophie moved into Spence's office for her one-to-one with Brenda, and this was one session that confirmed Brenda's presence was needed.

Sophie had been affected by the events of the session. She was exhausted and as she slumped down into the chair, lost grip on her handbag sending its contents spilling onto the floor. She looked down at the mess and was near to tears. Brenda gave her a reassuring smile, told her not to worry, and helped her retrieve everything before placing a well-needed cup of tea in front of her.

Spence had left with Fielding for a meeting with Merriman, and at the top of the agenda was feedback on the visit to Donald Fallows.

"I take it you didn't get the result you hoped for?"

Fielding sighed in frustration, "I did my best, but the man won't budge. Williams must be a terrifying individual, because Fallows is being beaten black and blue on a daily basis, yet he still won't give him up."

"What inducement did you give him?"

"As much as I was able. A single cell in Broadmoor."

Merriman looked surprised, “Broadmoor? Surely that would be a last resort for anyone. Hardly an enticing prospect.”

“It is if you fear for your life every day.”

Merriman glanced at Spence, who appeared to be just as stunned.

“There are obviously people in Broadmoor whom he fears more than the beatings.”

“No. I think it’s because once you’re there, it’s bloody near impossible to get out.”

“And Fallows thinks he’s going to get out! The man is deluded,” declared Merriman.

FOURTEEN

Tuesday 18th December – 07:00

In the CID office, Chris Sparkes sat staring out of the window, oblivious to the hubbub of changeover, or the phone that had been ringing persistently on his desk. His thoughts were not on work but fixed on a visit to Sophie that he'd made on route to the station. He wanted to see if she was okay, after all, he hadn't seen her for several days. He was missing his partner, and the time apart had made him realise just how much he appreciated her and wanted her in his life. He was smitten and had planned to roll up with a bunch of roses at the weekend. But on hearing that she was sent home earlier than usual from her shift, assumed she would have slept through the night, and been awake if he called in the morning.

He had knocked, rung the bell, and even called through the letterbox, before realising that her car wasn't in the drive. Where was she? He knew she couldn't be with her family, as having secured a council exchange, they now live in Dorset. And as far as friends go, he was sure she had some, but he didn't know who they were. Could she have stayed overnight with one of them?

Chris was still deep in thought when Jake arrived,

"What's up buddy?" sniffled Jake. Discarding yet another tissue into the bin. "This bloody cold, just won't shift."

Chris rallied, but it was evident that his mind wasn't on the job. His concerns about where she might be, or who she might be with, caused his stress level to rise.

"It's not that highly-strung woman of yours is it? She's a bloody nutcase."

Jake's ill-timed, flippant comment, lighting the touch paper and setting off an uncharacteristic overreaction to a harmless remark, "Why?" he demanded, "What did you do?"

"Calm down mate. Nothing. All I said was, are you okay, and she almost bit my head off. Bloody women, they're all unfathomable."

"When? When did this happen?"

"Yesterday afternoon when I was leaving. I guess, she was just coming on shift. Why?"

Chris shrugged, "It's nothing. Don't worry."

"It must be something mate. Come on, spill the beans."

Chris relented, "It's just that I turned up this morning, just before six, and she was out."

A smile grew across Jake's face, "She's a young woman." And gave him a knowing wink.

"No." he protested. "She's not like that. It doesn't feel right."

"Have you called her?"

Bristling at what he saw as a ridiculous question, "What do you think?"

"All right! That's enough! There's only so much shit I'll take, even from you." Pointing to the nameplate on his desk to remind Chris of his rank.

The fact is, Jake wasn't concerned at all. In his head, he suspected she'd just spent the night with another bloke and wasn't prepared to lock horns with him about it. After a moment spent allowing the temperature between them to cool, Jake suggested that if he couldn't make contact by lunchtime, they should both take a trip to her house, which Chris reluctantly agreed to.

"In the meantime, we need to pay another visit to Darcy. The DCI wants us to make some enquiries while that Mancini woman is here with Spence."

"What are we looking for?" Chris asked in a tone

suggesting it was a huge inconvenience.

Jake's eyes flashed, "Anything interesting we find in her office – is that all right with you?" came the snarky reply. "And it's what are we looking for Sarge!"

Perhaps Jake was now experiencing the negative side of being too easy-going. Can you remain as one of the lads and still command the respect of a higher rank? Time will tell.

09:00

Sammi Mancini and Jasmine arrived at the station and were shown to an interview room. Spence and Fielding were observing them through the glass.

Spence had met Ms Mancini before and found her to be very likeable. Fielding had not met her, and based on his past experiences with social workers, had a particular image in his mind of what she would look like - having always found them to be environmentally aware, and dressed to be comfortable. It was therefore a surprise for him to see this woman enter the room, contrary to his expectation.

She wore six-inch heeled, black patent shoes, and a black pinstripe tailored skirt suit. The jacket sporting double-breasted gold metal buttons, giving the impression of someone in authority. She had a warm and approachable expression, wore very little make-up, was petite and sat demurely, perched on the edge of the chair, pulling the pleat at the side of her skirt to allay the exposure of any flesh.

Jasmine, in contrast, looked pale against the black of her jogging suit. The bottoms were so long that they almost swallowed her white trainers, the top was zipped up to the neck, and her long hair was barely visible under the large hood. Mancini asked her to pull it down, but she refused, and sat with her arms tightly crossed in front of her.

Both officers had extensive experience with uncooperative

teenagers and were prepared for the usual start. It would begin with a refusal to answer any questions, followed by some form of encouragement by the appropriate adult, and then develop into a series of belligerent yes and no answers. In other words, they were both prepared for the task of getting blood out of a stone.

They had decided that it was paramount to get Jasmine onside as soon as possible. And to that end, made a further decision not to enter the room with a handful of documents. They wanted her to be comfortable and not feel threatened by officialdom, which also dictated how Fielding would greet them, on his own at first, making general chitchat before Spence joined in.

They both looked up as Fielding entered. His broad smile and outstretched hand made a good impression on Ms Mancini, and a flicker of acknowledgement with a shuffle in her seat by Jasmine.

"Thank you both for finding the time to come in. I know what's happened is something you would rather forget," he said. Placing a water bottle in front of Jasmine. "But we do need to ask a few more questions to help us find out what happened to Gemma."

Mancini picked up the bottle and moved it closer to Jasmine,

"We will do whatever is needed officer, to help find Gemma's killer."

Her last word caused Jasmine to wince. This was not the reaction Fielding wanted and was now concerned that his good work was going to be immediately undone by Ms Mancini's insensitivity.

Spence now entered the room. Mancini smiled up at him, "It's nice to see you again."

Spence nodded, and shook her outstretched hand, "You too." Then turned to Jasmine, "And how are you young lady?"

She didn't reply. Spence hadn't expected her to.

Fielding began the questioning, "Jasmine, tell me what it's like living in Darcy House."

She shuffled further into the seat. Mancini encouraged her to answer by tenderly stroking her arm and telling her all would be okay.

"It's all right," she answered begrudgingly.

Fielding aware that he was leaning in, pushed his chair back and crossed his legs, "What do you like best?"

Jasmine's eyes were a flood with suspicion, "My room. I suppose."

Fielding smiled, "Your room is next to Gemma's, isn't it."

"You know it is." The teenager's arrogance in full swing.

Yes, he did and didn't mind her hostile attitude towards him, at least she was speaking.

"Okay," he said firmly. "You're not a stupid girl, so I won't treat you like one, "How friendly were you with Gemma?"

She threw him a look of disgust, "What does that mean?"

All in the room under no illusion that she knew very well what it meant – she was just being difficult.

Spence had heard enough and used a different tack, "My daughter's mates text each other all the time, and lounge about in each other's rooms, talking about boys and stuff." Then pulled that adult, oh my God, face. "That's being friendly Jasmine. Is that how it was with you and Gemma?"

Jasmine allowed herself a half-smile, "Yeah, we did all that."

"And who else was Gemma's friend?" asked Fielding.

She didn't like that question, pulled her hood even lower down so her face was barely visible. Or was it perhaps that she didn't like Fielding?

He tried again, "It's okay Jasmine. You won't get anyone into trouble. Was it Sean McKinney?"

Jasmine looked to Mancini.

"It's okay, you can answer," And gave Jasmine's hand a little squeeze.

She crossed her legs and proceeded to bang her foot repetitively on the leg of the table. It was very irritating. Mancini buckled first and put her hand on Jasmine's leg to hold it still. Fielding made no comment. He just waited patiently for her answer. There was no way he was giving in.

"Would you like me to repeat the question?"

"No. she whined. Then let out a loud sigh of defeat. "Sean wasn't allowed in the building. He was banned by Mr Taylor."

"Do you know why he was banned?" asked Spence.

Her eye's flashed, "Taylor said, because he sold drugs."

Fielding turned to Mancini, "Were you aware of this?"

"Yes, I was. I also made sure that the boy didn't gain entry."

"But you did see him outside of Darcy, didn't you Jasmine?"

She looked surprised at the question and hesitated before answering, "No."

Fielding gave a knowing nod, "I think you did, because all three of you were seen at the nail parlour."

She pulled herself up in the chair, "How do you know that?"

"It's not important how we know. Don't worry Jasmine, you're not going to be in any trouble. But were you and Gemma with him in the park on Wednesday the fifth of December?"

Jasmine pulled her sleeves down over her hands, and wrapped her arms around her,

"If I tell you," she blurted out, "will you promise I won't go to prison?"

"Yes Jasmine, we just want the truth. I think you may have smoked weed together on that day. Am I right?"

She nodded. Spence described her action for the tape.

"And did Sean have an argument with the warden?"

She nodded again.

"Yes or no please Jasmine."

Looking up to the heavens, she huffed and replied, "Yes."

"And where did you all go when you left the park?"

"Don't know."

Ms Mancini it seemed had also now had enough,

"Answer the policeman Jasmine, for goodness sake, he's told you you're not going to get into trouble. Now, stop being so silly and start cooperating."

Jasmine appeared startled at her outburst. This was obviously out of character, and it had an effect. She sat up, pushed her hair away from her eyes, and looked Fielding in the eye,

"Gemma and me went back to Darcy. I think Sean went to work."

"Great!" said Fielding. "Thank you. Do you know where he worked?"

"No. But it was something to do with looking after dogs."

Fielding was excited. Williams had dogs, lots of them.

"Do you know what type of dogs?"

"No. Sorry."

"That's fine. You're doing really well Jasmine. Now, I want you to think back to Thursday the sixth of December. What did you and Gemma do that day?"

"In the morning we went to the market, and then Gemma left to go away for the weekend."

Spence smiled at Jasmine, "We know she went to stay with Sean. Do you remember if she told you where that was?"

"No. Only that it was where his boss lived."

"With the dogs?"

"I'm not sure."

He now pulled a photo from his pocket, "Do you know this man?"

Jasmine looked hard at it for some time. Fielding was beside himself waiting for her answer.

"Yes. I think I do."

"Really!" exclaimed Mancini. "Where from?"

Fielding raised his hands, indicating that he wanted her to stop contributing to the questioning, "It's ok Ms Mancini. Now Jasmine. How do you know him?"

"I saw him at the nail parlour."

Spence asked, "Nailicious! Are you sure?"

"Yes, he was talking outside to Sean."

The look on Fielding's face was a picture. He knew his warrant was signed and sealed.

"Have you ever seen him at Darcy House?"

"No."

Spence then turned to Ms Mancini, placed the picture in her hands and asked, "Have you?"

"No." she said quickly. And placed the photo back on the table.

Fielding now made his excuses and left the room, leaving Spence to finish the interview. He was keen to find out if Jasmine had seen the black van coming and going. She said that she hadn't, and Spence believed her. After all, it came and went when they were all in the daily meetings. However, he remembered that Gemma and the shepherd had made physical contact and wanted to press Jasmine on who else visited Darcy.

"Jasmine, just a few more questions. Did you see any adults visiting Gemma's room?"

"That's against the rules," declared Ms Mancini.

"It may be, but I'd still like to know. Did anyone break the rules Jasmine?"

Mancini looked very uncomfortable and began fidgeting in her seat. Jasmine recoiled and shook her head. Leaving Spence to assume that she did know something but was afraid to say.

"I think if the residents had seen anyone, they would have told me." claimed Mancini.

"Not if you weren't there."

"Excuse me?"

"You weren't there the weekend when Gemma was picked up and murdered, were you?"

"I. I was on leave."

"In Scotland?"

"Yes. Yes, on leave in Scotland."

"But you told me you had been on a course?"

Mancini was red in the face, "You must have been mistaken."

Spence is never mistaken and knew now that she was hiding something.

Jasmine looked confused, "You never said you went to Scotland."

"Well, I did. And with all that's happened, I probably forgot to mention it."

"Where in Scotland?" asked Spence.

"A place called Cainryan. I doubt you've heard of it."

But Spence had, "It's where the ferry comes in from Larne in Ireland. I know it well. What was the attraction for you?"

"I have friends who live there."

Spence knew his questions were proving uncomfortable, but there was little else he could ask at this point. Not until they know if Mancini was really Samantha Mann. Then he would have a multitude of questions to ask.

"Tell me Ms Mancini, what role did James Wilson have at Darcy?"

"That weirdo," blurted Jasmine.

Mancini leaped to his defence, "Shh Jasmine, that's unkind. The man is deceased."

Jasmine turned and faced her full on, "You know he's a weirdo, you said so yourself."

Mancini looked like she wanted the floor to swallow her up. Now is when she would have preferred Jasmine remained quiet. Her embarrassment was clear to see,

"He was a snoop, Inspector. Always peering at people. Unnerving people with his presence. He did odd jobs for Taylor. Awful jobs that nobody else liked to do."

"Such as?"

"Cleaning out the toilets and the outside storeroom."

"Did he clean the outside storeroom on Friday the seventh or Saturday the eighth?"

"I expect so, he only worked weekends."

Spence now had a good motive for his murder. He must have come across Gemma's body when he was cleaning. But why didn't he report it?

At that point his mobile buzzed, it was a text from Jake. They'd finished their search and were on their way back.

Spence could now end the interview, but if Sammi Mancini was Samantha Mann, then he'd be seeing her again very soon.

FIFTEEN

Tuesday 18th December – 14:00

The report on Chris and Jake's visit to Darcy was a detailed account of their actions and findings, and even though they believed the mess in the office suggested someone might have been there before them, they struggled to fill half a page. Fielding had hoped they would find some reference to Williams in Mancini's files, but if it was there, they couldn't find it. Spence wasn't at all surprised. He saw it as a fishing expedition at a time when Fielding was desperate for a reason to secure that search warrant. But now Jasmine has provided one, their trip to Darcy will be explained away as a mere dotting the I exercise.

Now back in the car, the officers were on their way to Sophie's house. Chris had tried calling and texting, but she wasn't responding. Jake had also tried her mobile, thinking she may be purposely ignoring Chris' attempts to contact her, but she wasn't picking up for him either.

Jake pulled up outside the house,

"See, I told you. No car. It's the same as when I came this morning. Even the curtains haven't been opened."

Jake felt the time was right to tell Chris the facts of life, even though he knew his reaction would be bad,

"Mate. You're not in a relationship, are you?"

"No. Why?"

"Because, if you're just friends, she won't expect you to be worried."

"What? What are you trying to say?"

"Mate. You've got no hold over her. She's out having fun.

Believe me, you're the last thing on her mind at the moment. Have a word with her when she comes on shift later."

Chris sat quietly, seething at the thought that Jake may be right.

"I'm going to try the door one more time before we go."

"Go on then," grumbled Jake. "But you're wasting your time." And proceeded to get out of the car.

"Where are you going?

Jake winked, "I'll look around the back."

Chris tried peering through the front window, but the curtains were drawn fully. He then proceeded to bang loudly on the door. There was no answer. He could hear Jake calling Sophie's name and going round the back to see what was going on, found him lying on the patio, with his head poking through the cat flap. Chris began to laugh. Jake pulled his head out and got to his feet. He wasn't laughing, and Chris could see by his pained expression, that something was wrong,

"What is it? What did you see?"

"I think you had good reason to be worried, the place has been turned over. Call Spence, let him know we're making an entry and to send a team."

Chris was shaking, and all fingers and thumbs as he tried to dial, missing a number before redialling, and getting through. Spence said he would respond on a blue light and be with them in fifteen minutes.

In the meantime, Jake had retrieved a hammer from his boot and was attempting to break the window in the back door. It was hard to break, being one of those panes of glass that had wire mesh inside, but eventually, he was able to put his hand in and undo the latch.

The sight was one that screamed an attack had taken place, and that Sophie had put up a fight. Lamps that had fallen from overturned side tables, lay smashed to pieces on the laminate. Plant pots and their contents were strewn about, the dispersed soil on the floor providing an insight as to the intensity of the struggle, and a tub chair laid up ended in the centre of the room, along with drawers that had been wrenched from the housing of a sideboard.

"Sophie!" they called out. "Sophie!" As they moved through the house in search of their colleague. Chris' heart was pounding as he ran up the stairs to check in the two bedrooms. Hoping to find her, but then terrified she would be lying seriously injured or dead.

"Clear," shouted Chris.

"It's clear down here too," yelled Jake.

They met up in the hallway,

"What the hell's gone on here?" asked Chris. Visibly shocked at the damage in the house.

"I don't know mate. It's madness."

The sirens could now be heard approaching and they walked outside to meet Spence.

"Is she inside?" he asked.

"No sir," replied Jake, "it's just like a bomb's gone off."

"Neither of you has touched anything, have you?"

"No sir."

With that, all three went inside to look at the scene again.

"Any trace of blood?"

"No sir."

"That's one good thing then, isn't it. I wonder what they were after?" Then turned to Chris. "Outside lad, we need to talk."

Jake was left to record the scene in his notebook, while Chris followed Spence onto the front lawn. They were about to have a conversation, when Spence noticed quite a large group of spectators had assembled and plumped for the privacy of his car instead.

"Now lad. I'm not blind or stupid. I know you and Sophie are more than colleagues."

Chris attempted to speak, he was going to explain that it wasn't the case, not yet anyway, when Spence raised his hand to stop him.

"I don't want to know, and as long as it doesn't affect your work, I don't care either. But I do care if it's a domestic situation responsible for this."

Chris was stunned. Spence was treating him like a suspect.

"I had nothing to do with this, sir."

"I understand you were at her door at five-fifty this morning."

Chris now realised that the gossip jungle drums had been at work in the station,

"Yes, I was, but I couldn't get a reply then either."

"So, whatever happened here, occurred between her arrival home the night before, and that would have been near to one in the morning, and before ten to six. Did you speak to her around one o'clock?"

"No sir."

"Did you speak to her or see her at any time yesterday?"

"No sir."

"Do you know any of her friends?"

"No sir."

"What about enemies?"

Chris shook his head, "Absolutely not sir." Then pondered on the way the questioning was going, and concerned with Spence's official tone, asked, "Do I need an alibi, sir?"

"Yes, lad. You do." Then turned to face him, "Do you have one?"

"Yes sir. I do."

"Good. What is it?"

"I stayed with a friend, a male friend, last night. We'd been to the boxing in Croydon, and I'd had a few drinks, so…"

Spence smiled, "Well for once the old booze has been a blessing. I will be checking it, of course, standard procedure and all that, but for now, you can partner with Jake. I want every piece of CCTV you can find."

The pair walked back into the house. Jake was chatting with the forensic team leader,

"They're about to blitz the place sir, so we should go outside."

"Before they do, I want to know if there are any devices, like a tablet or laptop amongst all this mess."

Chris told him that she had a laptop. That it was brand new – she'd only bought it the week before.

"Right. All of you, listen up. I need to know immediately if you locate a laptop, or any device come to that. I'll be back at the station if you come up with anything."

16:30

After hearing that Sophie was missing, Sarah arrived early for the evening chatroom shift. She wanted to help in the search, but Spence needed her to keep the momentum with the shepherd. She understood, but it didn't stop her from feeling useless. The shift was supposed to start at six o'clock, but she decided to log in early, at least it would take her mind off it.

She had just sat down, when Ron came rushing in, he was flustered, "Is it right that DC Sophie Steele is missing?"

"Yes, Ron."

He was agitated and pulled up a chair to sit beside her, "What happened?"

"No one knows yet I'm afraid. It's all such a worry."

"Well, I know something, and I'm not sure if I should say."

"What is it, Ron? Is it something to do with Sophie?"

"Yes, it is, but I don't want to get her into trouble."

"Ron. We need to know." She was dumbfounded that he would even think it was a good idea to keep secrets. Perhaps he was sweet on Sophie, he did pay her a lot of attention, and that could have influenced his decision.

Ron looked embarrassed, "I should have said something before."

Sarah was getting impatient, "Say it now Ron. Now. Please."

He went on to explain that two nights ago when he checked the chatroom feed, he noticed that Sophie had logged on after her shift had ended. And that he'd just checked it again, and she'd also logged on after her shift the previous night.

"So, she was contributing to the chat when she got home? Is that what you're saying?"

"Yes and no. She'd logged on but didn't contribute to the main chat. She was either just watching, perhaps she couldn't sleep, or was having private chats."

Sarah felt a chill run down her back,

"I'm not very techy Ron, but if she used her own laptop, could her IP address be traced?"

"Yes. If her laptop was on, connected to the one that is carrying out the trace and doesn't have a proxy server or VPN concealing it."

"And how easy would it be, to find out that she was a police officer?"

"If they're good at what they do, they could hack into her laptop, and get all the information off there."

Sarah was staggered, "Dear God! I know her laptop was a new one, and she's been so busy, she may not have set up the protection properly."

Ron was frantic and wringing his hands, "I knew I should have told someone the first night it happened, I'm so, so sorry."

Sarah didn't reply. What could she say? He was right, he should have reported it.

She now had to inform Spence of what Ron had told her.

Hurrying down the stairs to the floor below, she could hear his voice long before she got to his office. He was on the phone barracking someone, obviously already in a bad mood, and had no doubt that this news would send him ballistic.

"What on earth did she think she was doing?" he bellowed in disbelief.

"I expect she was trying to make headway with the shepherd," suggested Sarah. "But the chatroom is anonymous, so I can't think why he would abduct her. It doesn't make sense; she was no threat to him. Not until they met up anyway."

"Do you think she met him?" asked Spence. Then thought about his question and decided that couldn't be the case. That it didn't make sense either, that he would meet her, then come back later, trash her place, and abduct her. Too farfetched. Anyway, she would have informed them of what she was preparing to do. She was taken by surprise and fought her abductor; he was sure of that.

"It does make sense Sarah if he said something by mistake in their private chats that would give him away." theorized Harris.

Now that did make sense to Spence, "Bloody hell! Bloody hell!" he yelled. He was angry with himself for letting Sophie take the job on. It didn't feel right from the start, and took his frustration out on the desk, planting a hefty thump on the blotter, before storming into the main office.

"Has any CCTV come in yet?"

"No sir," replied Jake. "And the house-to-house is proving fruitless because everyone was asleep."

"What about her bloody car? Any luck tracing that?"

"Not yet sir."

"What are they bloody looking at?" he yelled. "There must be cameras all down the main roads. Tell them to look for any car passing at the same time, a black van comes to mind eh, or a bloody white Mercedes."

"Yes sir. It is all in hand."

"Then get me some bloody results!"

It was then that Fielding burst through the door waving his search warrant,

"I've got a team together; we're going to Williams. If he hasn't got Sophie, then I bet he'll know who has."

Spence thought Fielding was barking up the wrong tree, but anything was worth a try.

"I'm assuming it will be an armed response."

"Yes and give me Hearn and Madden. I'll need their muscle on this one."

Fielding, choosing to side line Chris because of his close relationship with Sophie. A man who would now be left to stew. Left to entertain hideous thoughts of her abduction, and worse, what pain she might be experiencing, and what horror she may be going through.

With the team all prepared, they made their way on a silent approach into the residential estate. Williams' house sat in the centre, on its own grounds. The walls were high, and the cameras a-plenty. So, unless the occupants were sleeping, which was unlikely at seven o'clock in the evening, they would see them approaching. The hope was, that under the cover of darkness, they wouldn't be noticed until practically on top of them. It would be then, that the fleet of squad cars would set off the sirens, and the raid commence.

Spence had stayed behind to manage the activity in the office and was listening to the events unravel on the radio. Fielding had made entry and while the officers conducted the search, he held Williams and his daughter in the lounge. Five minutes passed before Fielding announced that the target was not on the premises, Sophie wasn't there.

Fielding would return some three hours later with news of

a haul of drugs, assorted weapons, and three individuals in custody: Williams, his daughter Claudia, and an older gentleman identified as Williams' father. There were no dogs on the premises and learning that Williams had sold his interest in the greyhound racing some three months before, they were unable to initiate a search on those premises.

In the garages, they seized two vehicles. A 2006 Bugatti W16 Mistral, not registered to Williams, and expected to have been stolen to order, destined for a foreign purchaser. And a 2016 Mercedes S Class, that was registered to him, both vehicles would be examined by forensics. His daughter did not have a vehicle due to being banned for drink driving the year before. They also seized all the laptops, tablets, and computers for examination. If Williams is the shepherd, or knows the shepherd, the IT boys would find the evidence.

23:15

Merriman had arrived at the station and a briefing was underway in his office. Fielding described the raid and what they had uncovered,

"The forensic team will be there for a while yet, and I'm sure we will find more evidence pertaining to the supply of drugs."

"Did you find any Fentanyl?"

He let out a frustrated sigh, "No, we didn't."

News that none of them wanted to hear.

"That doesn't mean to say that he didn't have any before, does it."

"No, I suppose not," replied Merriman. Unconvinced, along with Spence, that Williams was their man for the murders. "How are your investigations progressing Spence?"

"Slowly, I'm afraid but everyone is doing their best."

"And has Sarah been online in the chatroom?"

Spence said she had, but the shepherd has not made an appearance.

"It could be because he's locked in a cell downstairs." declared Fielding.

"Then we need to question him soon Dave."

"If only. We're having to wait for his bloody solicitor."

It was now that a knock came on the door, it was Harris,

"You have news?" asked Merriman.

"Yes sir. DC Sophie Steele's car has been identified on CCTV."

With the news, the meeting ended abruptly as all three hurriedly made their way to the CID office. Chris was sitting alongside a technician on the computer, who was clicking through images that caught the car as it travelled along the main roads.

"This is her car, here sir," Pointing to the screen at a mini clubman travelling along the A234 towards Anerley. "She then turns left onto Anerley Road, which is the A214, and continues along until she gets to Penge Road, and onto the A213, where we lose her. Geoff, the technician is now searching through the cameras to see where she went."

All watched intently as he clicked and flipped from one screen to another until he laboured on one in particular. He pointed to the top of the screen,

"I think that's the mini, just turning into the approach to Norwood Junction station."

"Where's she gone now?" asked Spence. As the car seemed to leave the road.

Chris was already on Google maps, "I think she's driven into the supermarket car park."

What time was it?" asked Fielding.

Geoff drew their attention to the top of the screen that showed three thirty-two.

"I don't suppose you can access the supermarket cameras, can you Geoff?"

"No. But I can contact them and ask for the recordings to be sent over to me."

"But that's going to take hours," complained Chris.

Fielding agreed, "He's right. Spence, you need to go to the car park now, and let's hope the car is still there."

Spence left to get his coat and car keys from his office, and Chris followed behind. He asked if he could join them. Spence was in two minds, but Chris had the look of a man desperate to be included in the search, and relented, "Come on then. Grab your coat but follow orders and don't do anything that will make me regret taking you."

01:35

Madden, Sparkes, and Hearn accompanied Spence to the car park, Bloom and Harris remained. Bloom monitoring the chatroom with Ron, and Harris continuing his research, digging into Sammi Mancini's life. All were in it for the long haul, and all had a good reason to rely on adrenaline to keep them going. Sophie was a good friend and a trusted colleague. She would never have given up on one of them, and they were not about to give up on her, but they all knew that time was not on their side, and they needed to find her soon.

Fielding had remained at the station. He would interview Williams as soon as his solicitor arrived. It seemed to be taking a while, but no amount of complaining would hurry things along. Williams knew he couldn't wriggle out of being charged this time, he was going down, no doubt about it, and would do his best to be as uncooperative as possible. Fielding was expecting it, and as standard procedure had to be observed and followed, he couldn't usurp the system, however much he wanted to.

Spence and his team were now on site at the car park. The car was parked in isolation at the top left-hand corner. Conspicuous because all other vehicles were parked alongside each other on the right side, providing easy access to the exit. The manager said that the car park was busy twenty-four-seven and wasn't surprised that nobody noticed how long it had been there. He hadn't taken any notice either, assuming it belonged to one of the new members of staff they had employed for the Christmas rush.

Until forensics were in attendance, all they could do was peer through the windows in torchlight. Sophie wasn't inside. It didn't appear that anything was out of place, and their torchlight was good enough to identify that no significant amount of blood was visible, but not if the amount was small, it would be down to forensics to find and confirm that.

Jake's attention was on the boot, "I think we need to open it."

"We do," agreed Spence. Gloved up, he tried the catch. It was locked.

The tension was showing on their faces and all three had begun to expect the worst, that Sophie would be found dead inside.

Chris banged on the lid, and began to shout," Sophie, can you hear me? If you're in there, shout, or bang on something. Sophie! Sophie!"

Spence pulled him away, they were attracting attention from the workforce who were now on their break, "It's no good lad. We'll have to wait for forensics to open it."

The sound of sirens approaching meant they could expect them imminently. It would take a few minutes for the forensic team to set up and cover-up, but soon enough they were ready to pop the boot. Everyone took a deep breath, Chris turned away, he didn't want to look, deciding instead to wait to hear the outcome from the others. If she was dead, he was worried that he might break down.

There was a loud, metallic click and the boot was unlocked. Spence and Jake helped it open and to everyone's relief, it was empty.

"All clear," shouted Jake.

Chris' legs went to jelly, and he felt sick, "Thank God." he muttered under his breath.

The forensic team made an initial examination and confirmed that no blood was detected in the car. They would now move the vehicle to their facility to complete the forensic investigation, and the three, washed-out officers would return to the station. Or so they thought, but Merriman had other ideas. His orders were to go home, get some sleep and come back refreshed at eight-thirty. None of them was happy about it, and for Spence, it was easier said than done. Handing an important case over, into the hands of another shift, was like abandoning a child. But he also knew that the CCTV from the supermarket most probably wouldn't be available until the same time anyway, and they could all do with some much-needed rest. So reluctantly they did as they were ordered.

SIXTEEN

Wednesday 19th December – 08:00

Spence was the first back at the station and went straight into a meeting with DI John Bennett, the night shift inspector. It was important that he thanked all the officers on his team for agreeing to work overtime until they arrived. As is the practice of handover, Bennett fed back on incidents that had arisen on his shift, which would now be the responsibility of Spence to progress, but unfortunately, he had nothing new to report on Sophie's abduction.

The others, bar Sarah, arrived at around eight-fifteen. She turned up a little later armed with a tray of bacon rolls, her thoughtfulness appreciated by all concerned. They were starving. Harris took his to his desk and got stuck in while opening his emails. One was from his contact in the Irish constabulary. He read it intently and punched the air!

"Sir! A breakthrough."

Not being a morning person, Spence was feeling a little tender, and not in the mood for any dramatics, "What is it Harris?" he growled.

Harris read from the screen, "Sammi Mancini has been identified as Samantha Mann, and has a record. She was charged with possession of a class A drug, that she stole from a pharmacy where she worked as a Saturday girl."

For Spence, it started to make sense, "That was why she changed her name. She wouldn't have got a job here with a conviction for theft and drug possession, especially class A. What was it? Does it say?"

"Yes. Heroin."

"Well done Harris. I want you and Sarah to go and visit Mancini. Ask her about her name change, and grill her about how she managed to get forged documents?"

"Wouldn't you want to do that here?" asked Jake.

"No. I want to catch her off guard. No appointment. No phoning ahead. Just turn up."

He then turned to Jake, "Has that CCTV arrived yet?"

But before he could answer, Fielding walked in with Geoff the technician, "We have them here. They've just come through."

Geoff opened his laptop to reveal the CCTV download from the supermarket. He clicked on a timeframe for three-thirty. There was a moment of stillness until three-thirty-two when the beam from a car's headlights appeared approaching from the entrance. The car travelled slowly over the car park and stopped in the top left-hand corner, facing the wall. Almost immediately the driver's door opened, and a figure dressed all in black got out. They all agreed by the stature and the gait, that it was most probably a male.

"Can you zoom in?" asked Spence.

"I'll try, but it's quite an old system they're using, and the functionality isn't there. The higher the zoom, the lower the clarity."

Gradually, he increased the zoom but was only able to achieve a grainy, foggy image.

"Follow him, where does he go?"

They watched as the figure walked briskly along the top of the car park, past the wheely bin, and darted behind the row of parked vehicles on the right, leaving the way he came in. All the time keeping his head down, buried into the neck of his jacket.

"Can you pick him up from there?" asked Fielding.

Geoff changed applications and brought up the council cameras, he found the time frame, and there he was, walking towards Norwood Junction station, the entrance a mere twenty-five metres away.

"What time is the first train?"

Chris was already on Google, "From Norwood Junction, the earliest I can find is to London Bridge at five, twenty-five."

"So, where's he going at three thirty-eight?"

The man appeared to stop just short of the station and step into a shop doorway where they lost visual. Everyone thought he must have gone inside. But no, after a short while his feet and legs could be seen, and it was clear that he'd sat down.

Jake suggested that he could be keeping out of sight until the station opens.

Spence could see the merits of his suggestion, "Go to five o'clock Geoff, I expect the doors will be open by then. Let's see if Jake is right."

Geoff fast-forward the images, and at five o'clock, the doorway appeared empty.

"Go back a bit," said Jake,

And there he was, at four-fifty, waiting outside the station door, and his face was visible.

"Gotcha! shouted Spence. And turned to Jake.

"Organise two officers to find out if he bought a ticket and where to. Tell them to visit each station on the route, and to take a copy of the CCTV image of him and ask if anyone saw him alight from the train. Then ask to see the CCTV for when the train pulled in. It's a long shot I know but it would be helpful if we knew where he was heading. Also, arrange for forensics to process the doorway for any DNA. And Chris, take a copy of that face, and find out who the bugger is."

They now appeared to be getting somewhere, but he was still none the wiser about Sophie's whereabouts. Did she leave her house with this man? Did he leave her somewhere before dumping the car? Which Spence now believed stunk of pre-planning.

10:30

Sarah and Harris were parked up along the street from where Ms Mancini lived.

Harris was recording date and time in his notebook, "What if she isn't at home? She might be at work."

"No. She's working from home while Darcy is still a crime scene."

"I'll be good cop today?" he announced.

"What? Harris, you can be weird sometimes. Anyway, what's wrong with being bad cop?"

"I can't do it as well as good cop."

Sarah rolled her eyes, "Then it's time you learnt. It's bad cop Harris today."

They exited the car and walked towards her house. It was the last property in a long row of Victorian, three-storey, double-fronted terraced houses, and being at the end stood on a much larger plot. They walked into a wide gravel drive. A small patch of grass was on the left surrounded on two sides by borders of green foliage and the odd winter pansy. There were three steps up to the highly polished, plum-coloured door. Harris raised an eyebrow at the ornate brass furnishings and drew Sarah's attention to two names engraved on a plaque. Ms S Mancini and Dr Ryan Duffy.

"I wonder what the connection is between this doctor and Mancini?"

Sarah shrugged her shoulders, "No idea. It doesn't state what type of doctor he is, does it? I'll ask when we get in."

She pressed the bell, and almost immediately the door opened. Ms Mancini was expecting someone because she opened up with a beaming smile, which was soon to dissipate into a frown when she recognised Harris.

"What do you want?" she asked bluntly.

Sarah looked to Harris to respond, but it was clear that wasn't going to happen, so Sarah took the lead,

"We'd like to come in and speak with you, Ms Mancini. There are a few more questions we need to ask."

"It's not convenient at the moment," came the impatient and harsh reply.

"It's important that we speak with you, and if you refuse, then we will have to ask you to accompany us to the station, and we will speak there." voiced Harris. His tone was both stern and officious.

Sarah was stunned and impressed in equal measure. Why he thought he was no good at bad cop, she couldn't fathom. He was brilliant. Mancini backed down, opened the door, and showed them into the reception room on the left.

Sarah perched on the edge of a cream leather sofa, pulling a cushion from behind her to allow her to sit further back. There were so many of the things, there was hardly any seat left,

"Do you live here on your own? Or does the doctor I saw on the plaque outside live here too?"

Mancini looked down her nose at her, "Actually he does, yes, but I can't imagine why you would want to know."

Sarah smiled, "Purely making conversation, no offence meant. What type of doctor is he?"

"Not a medical one." she answered coldly.

"Ah. An academic one? And what's his specialism?"

Mancini was reluctant to answer, but as they were police officers, thought she should be forthcoming, "He's a research chemist."

Sarah's eyes widened and Harris momentarily stopped writing in his notebook. At this moment in time, any occupation drug related was going to pique their interest.

Sarah tried to keep it casual, "Oh that's a good line of work to be in. Is he here?"

She was biting her lip, perhaps trying hard not to be rude, "No. He's away. Are you sure it's me you want to talk to?" she asked sarcastically.

Sarah chose not to reply.

Mancini then cleared some documents off the coffee table, that Sarah had noticed were case studies, and offered them both a drink. Sarah said that she'd like a cup of tea, she felt it would keep them there for a little longer and give her time to look around. Harris declined. He would have loved one, but as a bad cop, didn't think sipping tea would give the right impression.

Mancini left the room and Harris allowed himself a smile. Sarah poked him in the leg, "You're such a liar."

"Ouch! I'm just doing as I'm told," he chuckled. And sat back into a red velvet, Chesterfield armchair, obviously enjoying the luxury experience. It certainly beat the second-hand recliner he bought off eBay.

Sarah looked around. She noticed that the items in the room were an eclectic collection. On one hand, there was one of those ornate French clocks on the mantle, she couldn't tell if it was genuine or not. Beside it was a photograph of a man smiling, holding up a glass of champagne. She looked closer, and the inscription on the silver frame identified that it was Dr Duffy. On the wall above it, was a painting by Picasso, she knew that it wouldn't be genuine but couldn't take her eyes off it.

Harris grinned at her, "You fancy that one, do you?"

She didn't answer. She was deep in thought and began taking an even closer look at her surroundings, and then back to the photo.

Harris, was bewildered by her behaviour, "What is it?"

"I know this room."

"What? How?"

And then she remembered, grabbed her phone, and started

taking images of the photo and the painting at different angles, then announced to Harris that they needed to leave.

"What?" he asked in disbelief.

She could hear Mancini coming along the hallway. "Come on. Get up, we need to go now!"

A second later, she entered the room holding a tray. On it sat two cups of tea and a plate of biscuits.

Sarah held a hand over her heart, "I'm so sorry to have put you through this inconvenience, but we've just had a call from the station. We have to get back straight away."

Mancini almost threw the tray down on the table, the tea spilling into the saucers. She was fuming, "I see. It certainly was an inconvenience, and I shall be speaking to Inspector Spence about this."

Sarah made their apologies again and left, almost breaking into a trot as she made her way back to the car.

"What is going on Sarah?"

"It's that room."

"What about it?"

"It's the same room in the photo that Gemma sent Jasmine on the Friday night."

Harris gasped, "Are you sure?"

"Positive."

"So, you think Mancini and the doctor had something to do with her death?"

"I do. We know that Mancini knew Gemma, and we can be pretty sure that if he's a research chemist, that he could get his hands on Fentanyl."

"But what could Gemma have done to end up being killed?"

"That's what we need to find out."

Harris asked to see her images and zoomed in on the photo of Duffy.

"Sarah. I think we may have stumbled on Sean McKinney's

killer too." And handed her the mobile, the zoomed image identifying that Duffy had a hair lip.

"Oh my God. Why was I in such a hurry to leave? We should have stayed to find out where he was. If you're right…"

"Of course I am," said Harris. "And that means Duffy could also be the shepherd! Call Spence now!"

Sarah's heart was in her mouth as she spoke to him. He told her to text the images, to stay in position, and that he would call back. The wait wasn't long, but it was torture, and both jumped when her mobile finally rang.

"Sarah. Both of you get back to the station. I've got officers on route to carry out surveillance on the house, and we've put out an APW on Duffy's car. I've also secured a search warrant, but I don't want to go in gung-ho and put Sophie's life at risk. And Harris."

"Yes, sir."

"DC Fiona Wells has cut her leave short to help in the search. She's keen and able. I want you to work with her and track down everyone that Ms Mancini and Duffy have affiliation with, work colleagues, casual friends, the lot, both here and in Ireland."

"We'll be back in half an hour sir, and I'll get on it straight away.

"And Sarah,"

"Yes, sir."

"Great work. Now go home and see your kids for an hour or so. I need you back for eight o'clock."

SEVENTEEN

Wednesday 19th December – 11:00

At the end of a muddy and pot-holed track, a mile from the main road in one direction, and nothing but fields for miles in the other, stood a traditional farmhouse. It held an isolated position. Far from the nearest neighbour, far from the prying eyes of the public, and for the best part of three years, its activities had flourished, far from the reach of the law.

Through leaded windows, the warm glow of home spilt out onto the courtyard, its cloak of respectability and deception illuminating the empty driveway. At the rear of the property, on hard standing and in the shadow of an imposing barn, stood the vehicle. The boot was open, and its cargo now delivered, lay motionless on the cold concrete, soon to be dragged into the barn, and left with the rest of the refuse being picked over by the resident vermin.

This barn was accustomed to welcoming visitors in the dead of night, to playing host to the desires of monsters. Its sturdy oak timbers were scarred with the trappings of evil and stained by the horrors of battle. A magnificent barn, built by pure-hearted men to store the fruits of their labour, now begrudgingly bore witness to man's greed and his ravenous appetite for blood.

Hay bales stacked one upon the other obscure the arena, the stage, the pit of doom. Discarded dog collars, broken canine teeth, and blooded fur swept up into a pile, wait to be cleared, ready for the next event. But tonight, it seems the pile will remain in situ. The decision being made that the fun needs to end. With the police on their tail, prudence dictated that tonight the barn will be razed to the ground. Evidence will no longer exist, prosecution will no longer be possible, and its latest visitor, Sophie, who now lies lashed at the ankle to the heavy metal ring of a trap door, will also perish in the inferno.

For a short while, she lay still and pathetic on the hard, blood-stained floor, in amongst the rubbish destined for disintegration. It would be the cold, boring its way through her skin to her bones, that would rouse her from her drug-induced sleep. Slowly, she opened her eyes and awoke into the darkness of a strange, unknown space that smelled of animals, of manure and of death.

She tried to push herself up off the floor with her hand, but her wrists were weakened and couldn't bear her weight. She winced in pain, and for a moment sat still in the dark. She was disoriented, unable to focus, her memories dreamlike, foggy, and unclear. What was this place? Why was she here? How did she get there?

Again, she attempted to stand but her legs felt heavy and lacked any strength, her shoe sliding across the sawdust denying any purchase with the floor. She was confused but determined to get to her feet. She tried again, and fell back again, unaware that her attempts were continually thwarted by the ropes that anchored her to the cold ring of steel. Frustrated, she reached out into the darkness but could find nothing to hold on to. Nothing to give her that little bit of leverage. Beaten and bewildered, she screamed for help, but nobody came. She was alone. Alone in the dark.

In the courtyard, two men stood listening to her calls for help. They smiled at each other,

"She's awake," purred the one with his hand clamped to his crutch.

"It's me first," snapped the other. Who pulled his hands from his pockets and took a few steps towards the barn door.

"Where are you off to?" shouted a voice in the darkness. It

was their boss emerging from the outbuildings, his two dogs trailing behind, "You've got work to do first, then you can have a bit of fun before it goes up."

Their ardour dampened, the men reluctantly followed him back into the darkness, into the stone-built store that housed the petrol.

EIGHTEEN

Wednesday 19th December – 20:00

The CID room was filled to capacity with officers chosen for the operation. With stab vests at the ready, they waited to be briefed. Spence was standing at the whiteboard with Harris, who looked drained having spent all of his time glued to a monitor. But the endeavour had been worthwhile, he and Fiona had discovered much to further the investigation. Spence had waited for Merriman to arrive and was now ready to start the briefing. Fielding was still in the bowel of the building with Williams and his ferocious solicitor and would catch up later.

Tonight we are travelling to the address on your paperwork in Brixton. The reason is that earlier today DS Sarah Bloom and DC Michael Harris, identified that the front room of the property, was the same room, in which Gemma Willis and Sean McKinney were pictured on the night Gemma died. The occupants of the property, Ms Sammi Mancini and Doctor Ryan Duffy are therefore prime suspects in her murder and that of Sean McKinney. We also have reason to believe that Dr Duffy is the individual called the shepherd and is now our prime suspect in the abduction of DC Sophie Steele. This man is not to be underestimated. He's dangerous and may be armed.

The background of this couple is important, especially for those officers searching through the paperwork. Their relationship began in Ireland when they both worked for a pharmacy in Cork and when she was known by her legal name of Samantha Mann. Following the completion of her one-year sentence for a drug conviction, the pair moved to the UK. We know that soon after entering the country, she changed her name to Sammi Mancini. This was not through deed poll, so be on the lookout for any paperwork that might suggest where she managed to acquire her forged documents, including her passport, and driving license.

Our primary goal is to find DC Sophie Steele alive and well. Leave no stone unturned in your search of the property, garage, and sheds. If you find anything at all that you believe could belong to her, or lead us to her, bring it straight to me.

We also need to find evidence of Gemma's and Sean's murders. All devices and hardware, plus anything else that you believe is relevant, including property or clothing should be bagged, recorded, and sent for forensic examination. I'm sure that Ms Mancini is still taking drugs, so be on the lookout for those stashed away too. With regards to the doctor, we expect he will have an office in the premises, and we have a forensic accountant in our number and a pharmacist, who will check that space for any evidence of Fentanyl, but I will also need all officers to search all rooms and all bins for any stock of the drug or used syringes,

The plan is for two squad cars to initially attend the house, DC Harris and I will be in one accompanied by armed officers. DS Bloom, DC Wells and DC Hearn will be in the other, and DS Madden will organise the deployment of officers to the side and rear of the property. On entry, all individuals will be arrested, secured, and transported to the station. I have already spoken with the officers responsible for that. The remainder of you, forensic officers and any other personnel will need to be parked up in close proximity, ready to respond when I give the order. Good luck everybody. We move at 20:45.

Pulling up outside the house, a light could be seen in the

upstairs window. Spence rang the bell. He could hear movement, and called out,

"Ms Mancini, it's DI Jack Spence." He knew she liked him and would not be afraid to answer the door.

He could hear her coming downstairs and shuffling in her slippers towards him. Then stopped to engage the security chain before opening the door. All he could see was her little face peeping around it. There was no sight or sound of Doctor Duffy.

He stood back, so as not to appear pushy, "Can I come in please?"

"It's late," she whined, "I was going to bed."

"Sorry. But it is important."

It had been a long day, she was tired, dressed for bed and still reeling about her earlier experience with the police,

"That's what your officers said earlier, but it wasn't." came the prickly reply.

Spence smiled, "Things go awry sometimes, don't they? But it is very important that I speak to you now."

He stood firm, she could see the determination in his eyes, and reluctantly slipped the chain and opened the door. Casually, he strolled into the hall. His right hand tucked behind his back clutching the handle of a handgun while he surveyed the surroundings for any movement,

"Is Doctor Duffy in?" he asked.

She was taken aback, she couldn't think why he wanted to know, "No. He's away. Why?"

Spence smiled down at her but didn't reply, which unnerved her. She became suspicious, tightened the cord around her dressing gown and started to distance herself from him. Dwarfed by his presence, she cowered as he asked if there was anyone else in the house.

Her wide eyes filled with fear, her voice trembling, "No. What is all this about?"

It was now that Spence holstered his gun, and on seeing the weapon, she reeled back in surprise. Spence sat her down on the chair beside the hall table, asked her to keep calm, and stressed the need for her to listen carefully as he produced the search warrant from inside his jacket pocket. This was the last thing she expected, and her shock was evident. Her eyes glazed over as he read from the warrant, and she learned that her partner was suspected of murder. It was a bombshell and the shock had left her speechless.

He asked her if she understood. She nodded her acknowledgement, and Spence, wanting to question her in quieter surroundings, walked with her to the kitchen. His idea being that if he spent some time speaking with her in the house, where she felt safe and more at ease, that she would be more likely to cooperate. Sarah was called in to sit with her.

The three of them sat at the kitchen table. The hum of the dishwasher providing a familiar and comforting backdrop to the alien situation she found herself in.

Spence leant back in his chair, "Tell me Sammi, where is Doctor Duffy?"

Using her first name, Spence hoped it would make the experience less formal. She seemed happy with it, and responded immediately, "Really, I don't know," followed up quickly with, "who is Ryan supposed to have murdered?"

Neither officer answered. Sarah moved closer to sit beside her, "Have you had a row?"

"No. Nothing like that," she insisted, "I'm sure he'll call soon and let me know where he is."

"Have you tried calling him?" asked Spence.

"Yes, but his phone is turned off." And as an afterthought added, "Perhaps he's driving?"

"Would anyone else know where he might be?"

Fiddling with the cord of her gown, she admitted, "I've tried everyone I know. Even the kennels."

Both Sarah and Spence thought the same, that calling your contact list was unusual behaviour if you're not worried,

"Kennels?" he asked. The reference to dogs had piqued his interest.

"Yes, he adores dogs. All types of dogs, but especially the Jack Russell. He's a part owner of kennels where they breed them. You know, for shows and things like that. We have two of our own, but he must have taken them with him."

This was significant news; it was a hair from a Jack Russell found on Gemma.

"Where are the kennels?"

Sammi reached up and took down an advertising card pinned to the board on the wall. For the next few moments, Spence sat quietly reading the card but was actually observing her. He was trying to develop his impression of her. He couldn't see her as a murderer and wondered what role she played in the whole, grubby and sinister set-up.

He looked her straight in the eye, "Has Gemma ever been here?"

She genuinely looked surprised, "No. Of course not. Gemma, why would she come here?"

Spence pulled the image from his jacket pocket. "This is Gemma, in your front room."

Her hands began to shake, and her eyes well up with tears.

"It is your room, isn't it?"

Engulfed in emotion, she could only nod in confirmation. It was clear that this photo, of a young girl in her home, was distressing to accept. It was also now clear who it was that Ryan was suspected of murdering. Spence knew that the penny had dropped and was waiting for the questions, but none was forthcoming. Surely she would want to know why Ryan was suspected of Gemma's murder. But the lack of questions left Spence suspecting that she didn't need to ask because she already knew.

"Do you know the boy in the picture?"

Holding the tissue to her nose, she snuffled, "Yes, it's Sean McKinney." And in a raised, angered voice added, "And I don't know why he's in my house either!"

"What can you tell me about Gemma's and Sean's relationship?"

"I caught them together in her room. It was obvious that he'd stayed the night." And with the questioning now focused on others, she seemed to gather herself, to reinstate her professional mien.

"I turned him out of course and warned her against seeing him again. He was bad news. He sold drugs you know."

It was then that Fielding walked in and announced that they'd found a laptop hidden in the wardrobe of the main bedroom. He placed it on the table. They gloved up and opened it,

"Is this yours?" he asked Sammi.

She shook her head, "No. I've never seen it before."

Spence started it up. It needed a password. Sarah suggested it could be one of the dogs' names. Sammi told them it was Flossie and Joey, but neither worked. Spence was getting impatient. The next step was to get Ron involved, if anyone could get in, it would be Ron. Sarah made the call.

Fielding moved his chair to sit opposite Sammi, "When did Ryan leave?"

She threw her hands up, "I don't know."

Not convinced she was being truthful, he asked firmly, "When was the last time you saw him then?"

She hesitated before answering, "The night before last."

"Did he have anybody with him?"

She looked puzzled, as if to suggest that to have people with him would be unusual, "No. Such as?"

"Such as two men?"

She shook her head rather than answer. Could this be

because she now had an idea what two men Fielding was referring to? The expression on the officers' faces suggested that they thought it might be the case.

"Do you know where Detective Constable Sophie Steele is being held?"

"What? God! You're talking in riddles. Who is that?"

Fielding glared at her. Was her alarm an act? He wasn't sure and was getting rattled - tapping his pen on the table in frustration at his lack of progress with this woman.

"Where would Ryan go when he goes away?"

She held her head and burst into tears, it was all getting too much, "I don't know."

Fielding, hardened by experience, and sceptical of women who weep to command, remained unaffected, "I understand from my officers that his car, a BMW five series, is still in the garage."

She sat upright in surprise, "Is it?"

"Does he have a second car?"

"No. But he does let his friend keep his car in the drive sometimes. He has a set of keys for it."

"And what make is it?

"It's a Mercedes."

"Colour?" he demanded abruptly, please and thank you, now completely done with.

"White." she answered warily. Clear by her expression, that she was in the dark as to why he wanted to know about other vehicles.

"And a black van, has he ever owned one or have access to one?"

She was about to answer but thought better of it, clammed up and looked down. Most likely concerned by the tone of the questioning and didn't want to make things even worse for Duffy. She may have thought she'd already said too much.

Fielding continued to press her for an answer, "Sammi?"

She twisted around on the chair to avoid his gaze.

"Sammi. Black Van!"

All three officers were staring at her, waiting for the answer. The tension was unbearable, and it was now that her shoulders dropped in surrender; she wasn't strong enough to maintain the fight. Choked up and mumbling, her reply was difficult to interpret, and Fielding asked her to repeat it.

Reluctantly and despairingly she answered, "The kennels have a black van."

Fielding was sure now that Duffy was their killer and asked Sarah to stay with Sammi in the kitchen while he and Spence left the room.

"Jack, we need a search warrant for the kennels, and ask DS Madden to lead a team to execute it."

"Yes sir. And what about Mancini? Do you think she's involved in the murders?"

Fielding shook his head, "I doubt it. Do you?"

"No, but I think she knows more than she's telling."

"I agree, get her removed to the station. Perhaps she'll be more forthcoming there."

Their attention was now drawn to the front door and the arrival of Ron. He stood in the hallway explaining his presence to some of the search team. One had just finished in the laundry room, and the others were bagging up evidence for transportation to the station. Fielding ushered Ron into the laundry room, and gave him the laptop with one simple instruction, to get them in. To one of the officers, he gave instructions to initiate an APW for the car, and the other to circulate a photo of Duffy to all constabularies. They then went off to check on the progress of the search.

The forensic expert and the pharmacist were in Duffy's home laboratory checking the inventory of his private stock of chemical substances, and two officers were systematically checking every drawer and cabinet in his office. Standing against the wall was a large cupboard, but on opening they were surprised to find the shelves were empty. Spence was sure that it should have been heaving with files. His one at home was, and he didn't have research records to keep. He went back to the kitchen to speak with Sammi, and asked if there was anywhere else that he kept paperwork. She suggested he looked for a filing cabinet in one of the outbuildings. He thanked her for cooperating and Sarah, knowing how difficult it must be for her, gave a reassuring smile,

"It's all very scary isn't it? Shall I make us both a nice cup of tea?"

She smiled back, "Yes. That would be nice." Sat further back in her chair, crossed her legs, and looked more comfortable. Sarah decided that now was a good time to probe her about Duffy.

"You must have been quite young when you met each other?"

"Yes. I was fourteen."

"Wow, that is young, because he's quite a bit older than you, isn't he?"

"Twelve years. But I knew straight away that we were right for each other."

"What did your family think about it?"

"I didn't tell." Her eyes flashed, "We just sneaked about until I was nearly sixteen."

"What happened then?"

This was one question too far, she clammed up, but Sarah was determined to get some answers. Placing a mug of tea before her on the table, she pulled her chair closer and sat alongside.

"We know about the drug charge Samantha."

Stunned at the comment, she embedded her face into her hands and sobbed.

"When is this nightmare going to end?" she pleaded. With the pretence no longer necessary, she was able to be herself and slipped into her true accent. Her Irish roots were now very evident.

"When we know the truth Samantha." Sarah handed her a clean tissue, "Here, dry your eyes, crying won't help."

She quietened down, blew her nose, and sighed, "I suppose I always knew this day would come. I told him it would, but he wouldn't listen. He never listens."

"What day Samantha?"

"The day I'm found out. The day my life will change."

"How will it change?"

"I'll lose my job for a start. And that will be one more reason for him to leave for good."

"So, the relationship is on bumpy ground after all?"

Sammi looked embarrassed, "It has been for about six months." She looked up at Sarah. "Do I have to say why?"

Sarah nodded, "It would be a good idea." Her expression clearly denoting yes; you do.

"It's just that… well… he doesn't find me attractive anymore."

"Has he said as much?"

"He didn't have to. He has someone else, or more than one for all I know."

Sarah was intrigued, "Go on."

"The bastard gave me Chlamydia! So he got it from someone, didn't he."

This was interesting to say the least. Now they had three people with the same disease, and this will be the link that binds them together. Who passed it to who will be a job for the pathologist? Sarah asked Fiona to sit with Sammi, so she could report the conversation back to Spence and Fielding.

The pair of them were now sitting with Ron. They were out of their depth, and completely in the dark as to what he was doing, nevertheless, they sat glued to the screen waiting for a eureka moment. Ron had obviously set something in motion because the screen was black, and white text of some sort was scrolling up at a rate of knots.

"What's all this about Ron?" asked Fielding.

"Do you want the long version or the short one?"

Fielding was in no mood for humour, "What do you think?" he snapped.

"Okay, sorry. I'm trying to bypass the password, and here we go, I'm in.

"Go to pictures Ron,"

Spence interrupted, "Actually, we'll take it from here." Thanked him and asked him to help with the transport of the other devices, of which there were many.

Now they were in, Spence was fine navigating the system, and if they came across images of Gemma, he certainly didn't want Ron to view them as well. Fielding took Ron's seat, and the pair went straight to folders. Each one was identified by a letter, a number, and a date,

"Any preference Dave?"

"Let's start at the beginning. The one marked A1 August 16."

Sarah now came rushing in, "Sir."

At the same moment, Spence had just seen the content of the folder, "Dear God!" he cried.

The images were so graphic and perverted, that they shocked this seasoned officer. "He's definitely our man. Sick bastard."

"What did you want Sarah?" asked Fielding.

She started to explain, "We know that Gemma had contracted Chlamydia, and Sammi has just told me that she had also contracted Chlamydia, from Duffy. So, it could have been that Gemma passed it to him, and perhaps it made him angry to think she gave it to him, or even jealous when he realised she was sleeping with someone else, and he killed her."

Fielding wasn't so sure, "There's a lot of girls on this laptop Sarah, and only one has turned up dead. It's not his MO is it?"

"We won't know if they're dead sir until we trace them all."

"I don't know." He wasn't convinced. "We need to take the laptop back to the station and view the photos there. It could be that these are third-party downloads, and not necessarily produced by the man himself."

"Before we do, just try that one, G2." urged Spence.

Fielding clicked on the file, and their victim Gemma was confirmed as one of his conquests. "There must be thirty or more photos and just as many videos," observed Sarah. "He was obsessed with her."

Fielding was getting anxious, "We need to go now Spence. This is not the place to view these." And called Ron in to package the laptop.

"Shall I just check the history before I close it down?"

"Yes. That's a good idea, it might give us a clue as to where he's gone."

At the top of the list was a web address and scrolling down showed that he had visited the site on numerous occasions, daily in fact, and sometimes more than once a day.

"What is it? A sex site or something?"

Ron said that he couldn't tell until he opened it.

"I'll give money that it's a Bloody chatroom," said Spence. And gave the instruction to open it up. It seemed to stutter and crash, then stutter again before crashing again. Ron shook his head and moved to close the browser.

"Wait," insisted Spence. "The page is loading, look!"

It was, but the progress was painful to watch. Slowly, tiny increment by tiny increment, it revealed its contents. Images of smiling men and women, adverts for exotic holidays, and dates for get-together nights. But their patience reaped rewards when the eureka moment they had all hoped for, materialised. Emblazoned across the top was written, 'Welcome Abram122'. Spence slammed a fist onto the table, "Now we have our proof. That bastard Duffy *is* the shepherd."

NINETEEN

Wednesday 19th December – 21:00

The effect of the drug was subsiding, and with it came the awful awareness of Sophie's situation. Recognition of her restraint had confirmed she was a prisoner, and her eyes now accustomed to the dark had revealed the surroundings to her. It was unfamiliar and frightening.

As she scanned the area, her eye was drawn to the low circular wall, she recognised the pit immediately and knew her captors would be cold-hearted men. Ones that thrive on the thrill of a kill, and ones that would show no mercy. If she wanted to survive, she would have to escape.

The first step would be to rid herself of the rope around her ankle. Then, perhaps she could find a way out. She pulled at it, but it was thick, and tied in a tight knot. She clawed at it, her nails tearing as she gripped and pulled at the twine. It wouldn't budge. She looked around for something on the floor that might help. Something pointed or something sharp. There was nothing. Nothing.

"Dear God!" she screamed. "Why me?"

It was then that a scurry behind made her jump. It would be rats taking an interest, and Sophie was easy prey. She had nothing and no one to protect her from an attack by these gregarious rodents. It was now imperative that she found a way to untie the rope. Panicking, she turned the pockets of her trousers inside out, perhaps she would be lucky and find a hair clip, but they were empty. She cursed at not wearing a belt that day, the buckle would have done it. The only other thing she had that was sharp, was her earrings. With trembling hands, she removed the stud, discarded the back onto the floor and pulled at the twine with the post. But it was soft gold and bent under the strain. She'd failed. All was lost. She had nothing else. Frustrated and angry, she threw the earring across the floor sending a rat scurrying after it. It was then that the thought of the rats around her made her shudder, and the base of her bra dug into her flesh. Of course, her bra.

Quickly she opened her shirt and lifted her breast out of the cup. Yes! It was wired. She now had a chance. She pulled at it, but it was sewn in, the only option was to bite at the fabric to make a hole and then she could pull the wire out. It worked. Triumphantly, she held the life-saving semi-circle of metal tightly in her hand. It flexed and wasn't rigid as she had hoped, but it was her only lifeline. It had to work.

Shuffling on her bottom she inched her way closer to her foot, where she hoped she'd be able to put her weight into the effort. Doubled over, and arms stretched out, she pulled at it with the wire, but each time it slipped out and over the top. She needed to get the wire secured behind one of the twists, then she could lever at it and loosen it. She was sure that once it was freed off, she could use her hands to untie it. But attempt after attempt proved fruitless, it wasn't happening. She tried to straighten the wire, first with her hands and then with her teeth, but it wasn't moving. It seemed everything was against her. It was then, beaten, and dispirited, sobbing into the crease of her arm, that she heard the voices of men.

Her pulse quickened, and fear engulfed her at the sound of the door opening up. They were coming in. Statuesque and breathless, she watched in horror as a beam of lamplight expanded its reach across the floor towards her. She cowered as they approached, and whimpered in sheer terror as they stood over her,

"Not so brave now are we Tammy16, or should I say, Detective Constable Steele." declared one of the men. It was

Duffy. His face was hidden behind the lamp that blinded her as she tried to look.

She pulled her legs in tightly and wrapped her arms around them. She didn't reply.

He laughed, "I've got two men here," Their lecherous grunts could be heard behind him, deep, grotesque and threatening. "And I've promised each of them fifteen minutes of fun," he paused, "with you. So, ready yourself, my sweetheart."

Sophie's heart was pounding hard as if it was trying to escape from her chest. But for her, there was no escape. Her rape at the hands of these morons was inevitable, it would be brutal and only minutes away. Dear God, was there no one to help her?

It was then that Duffy's attention was drawn to the ring of his mobile. The men moved forward,

"You go first," said one to the other, "I like to watch."

Duffy, it appeared, was now in the midst of an argument. The men took no notice, and he, in turn, was oblivious to their actions. One sat on a hay bale, put his hands on his thighs, and was getting comfortable to watch the show. The second man, stockier and who reeked of beer and cigarettes, kneeled beside her. His face contorted with a licentious and predatory smirk. He grabbed and pawed at Sophie's legs. She punched him in the head persistently and tried to push him off, but he was relentless, forcing himself upon her and prised the zip on her trousers open. He was strong and resisting was painful. He grasped her waistband firmly, and wrenched her trousers down, taking her pants along with them. She lay exposed and at the mercy of these men. She was terrified, she was weak, her screams pathetic, yet she fought bravely against the force of his hands prying her legs apart. It was then that he realised it was either cutting her trousers off or cutting the rope, something had to happen before he could move inside her.

His mate, knife in hand, gestured that he would cut the rope. Sophie's heart sank, she knew then, that by gaining her freedom from her restraint, she would lose her soul to this beast of a man and fought hard against it. She thrashed and clawed at his face, squirmed, and wriggled, but he just laughed, it seemed he enjoyed the fight. He was determined and strong. She was weak and getting weaker. Her body finding it harder and harder to resist, and when all her strength was spent, she let out a piercing scream as her legs parted,

"That's it, about fucking time," he shouted. Then turned to his mate, "Come on give us a hand."

The man came over and knelt behind her head. He smelt of body odour and beer, and pulled her arms away, holding them tightly at the wrists, while his mate undid his flies.

"Now, hold her there till I'm done," he ordered.

Excitedly, and drooling, like a rabid animal, he dropped his trousers and lay over her, smothering her, his bulk so heavy, she could hardly breathe. It was then that Sophie had given up all efforts to resist, she just wanted it over and done with, and lay sobbing while he laid upon her. It was also when Duffy came back in and ordered them both to follow him.

"What!" shouted the rapist, "Not fucking now!"

"Now!" screeched Duffy, "she'll still be here when you get back."

He was snorting like an irritated bull, his saliva dripping onto her neck. Unable to find the words, he thumped the floor in anger, sending sawdust flying into her eyes. She could feel his body shaking with rage as he climbed off her, pulled up his trousers and stormed off with an exaggerated swagger, aggression oozing from every pore of his body. The other man, who was still kneeling on the floor, pushed her over onto her front, fondling her breasts and fingering her pubic area before re-tying the rope, then whispered in her ear, "Keep it warm for me bitch." And followed his mate out.

Sophie was saved for now, and let out an emotional and deep, visceral cry of relief. She was safe from the rapists but for how long. In the courtyard, the men were having it out,

"You said fifteen fucking minutes!" he screeched. Enraged and with fists held high, he threatened to land a punch.

Duffy stood his ground. He was fearless and wielded his superiority like a sword to subdue him, "I know what I said! You will get it! Just not now!"

"Why?" he snarled.

"Because a delivery of petrol is due any minute, that's why, and I need the dogs taken to the kennels. I can't risk them going up with the barn."

"And why have *we* got to do that?"

"Because brothers, I said so."

TWENTY

Wednesday 19th December – 23:00

Sammy Mancini was now in the custody suite being processed. She had refused to answer any more questions and would spend the night in a cell. A formal interview, accompanied by her solicitor, had been scheduled for the morning.

The search team had also returned with their haul for forensics, and Spence's team, who refused to sign off shift, were back in the CID office trawling through the household documents retrieved from the property. They didn't care about the time it took, getting their colleague back was the only thing on their minds.

Harris scratched his head, "What are we looking for?"

"I don't bloody know," admitted Hearn. "Anything that might tell us where he's taken Sophie."

Whilst they searched for that golden nugget, Spence was with the IT department examining the laptop, when his phone began to ring. It was Chris Sparkes.

"Sir, the man at Norwood Junction station is Gerry Brady. He's from Ireland and the stepbrother of Dr Duffy."

"Well done lad. Check with the pathologist, see if the DNA is ready so we have two forms of identification, and pass this on to DCI Fielding. Ask him to call his contacts in Ireland. I want an address for this man and see if you can find out what lowlife he hangs with. We need that second man."

In the meantime, the team had now moved to Spence's office so as not to interfere with DI John Bennett's night shift again. Out of work, he was the life and soul, but on duty, a totally different animal. An irascible man: woe betide anyone that caused interruption and disruption to his working practices.

Sarah had pulled rank and bagged prime position behind the desk, while the others sat awkwardly around the edges. Harris, who had struggled with documents that balanced precariously on his bony knees, had lost patience and rehomed Spence's treasured desk belongings to the top drawer of the filing cabinet, giving him space on the table.

"He won't like that Harris!" warned Sarah.

"Is it me or are we missing something?" asked Hearn.

Sarah looked up from her pile of invoices, "Illuminate us."

"Sophie's laptop hasn't been found, has it? So he's either taken it or got rid of it."

"That makes sense," agreed Harris. "But he could have done that anywhere. What are you thinking?"

"I'm thinking that if we had the laptop, Ron could find evidence of her chat with the shepherd, and I'm also thinking that nobody thought to check the wheely bin at the supermarket. That guy could have put it in there as he passed by."

Sarah looked alarmed, "Are you kidding me? You'd have seen him."

Hearn shook his head, "No. The CCTV pictures were really bad, it was hard to see even the car!"

Sarah pointed to his mobile that lay on the table, "Ring Chris, he might know."

But he didn't need to, Chris had just arrived with pizzas courtesy of DCS Black. On one of the boxes was written, for those who have no homes to go to, your service is greatly appreciated.

Hearn looked at them longingly but had a feeling he wasn't going to get to eat one.

"Hey, Chris. Did anyone search the wheely bin at the supermarket?"

"I don't remember anyone doing it."

Sarah could not believe what she was hearing, "Right, both of you, get down there now. I'll update the boss."

Spence was with Fielding listening to the operation at the Kennels. Jake had gained entry and it sounded like all hell had broken out. His voice was barely audible amid the cacophony of barking, yelling and sirens, and both officers were glad they were sitting out on this one.

"Sir. Sir," called Jake.

"Yes, we can hear you," replied Fielding. "Is the van there?"

"Yes sir. It's here."

Fielding slapped Spence on the back, "We should get down there."

Spence reminded him that Jake was once a DI, that he was capable and knew what to do.

"I just hope it's the van we're looking for," said Spence.

"Get on to forensics, and ask them to rush it through, we need to know if Gemma was inside."

Jake was now back on the radio, "I'm bringing in four individuals for questioning, two you will be very pleased to see, Mr Gerry Brady, along with his brother Connor Brady."

"Yes! We've got the bastards!" shouted Spence.

Jake continued, "Also, the manager of the kennels, Stuart Weisman, and his wife, Kathy Weisman."

Both men shouted in unison, "Great work Jake!"

"We also need animal welfare down here, as there's nobody left to look after the animals. There are twelve dogs, two are the Jack Russell breed, but the rest look like illegal breeds to me, and two of those are due to welp."

"I'll see to it lad. Well done!" said Spence.

And as one call ended, another came in. This time it was Sarah, and for Spence, his elation turned on a sixpence to despair when he heard of the mistake. And responsibility for that lay squarely with him. Perhaps he wasn't perfect after all, perhaps he was getting past his best. Retirement had been on his mind, but if the laptop is found in the bin, he might not get the chance to hand his papers in, they may be handed to him.

The next half hour was stressful for everyone as they waited for the call. If they found the laptop it could prove to be a turning point in the investigation. If they didn't, then they were back to square one. Regardless of the outcome, for Spence, there would be consequences. All eyes were on the clock on the wall, it seemed to be going slower than usual, and each thud of the minute hand punctuated the silence and added to the tension in the room.

At last, Spence's mobile rang. It was Hearn. They had the laptop. Immediately after hearing this, he wasted no time organising a team to conduct a thorough search of the bin. The boys did have a look and said that they couldn't identify anything they thought would be useful to the enquiry, but Spence wasn't going to take any chances.

Once back at the station and dusted for prints, the laptop was handed over into the waiting hands of Ron. Everyone was getting geared up for the news, but Ron was concerned about their enthusiasm because he'd anticipated that the device would be damaged in some way and that retrieving the information may be a lengthy job. But the laptop was pristine, as new as when she bought it the week before. He opened it up, and the folders were accessible, so too, evidence in the history of her activity. It identified the chatroom website, but no records of her chats could be found. Ron, therefore confirmed that the laptop did indeed, have all the security controls installed, and that it had not been subject to hacking.

Spence, with hands clenched tightly behind his neck, paced up and down,

"How the bloody hell did he know? If he didn't hack, how did he know where she was?"

The others were thinking the same, nobody could answer him, until Harris had a thought,

"If he didn't hack into her laptop, then the only answer is that he was tipped off. Someone told him what she was doing."

Spence stopped in his tracks. He knew that would make sense, but the scale of the investigation would be massive.

"The whole bloody station knew what was going on. It would be like finding a needle in a bloody haystack."

Harris stood his ground, "I disagree. I think we can discount any and all officers. I don't believe that any one of us would betray a colleague."

Sarah, Hearn, and Chris all supported his comment,

"So, who's left?"

"Who else was in the room?" asked Harris.

Sarah looked to Spence, "Well, there was us, Ron and Geoff…"

Ron spoke up immediately, "It wasn't us. I can assure you all of that."

"Then the only other person present, and who had a close professional relationship with Sophie, was Brenda Watson. What do we know about her?"

"Nothing!" said Sarah. "And she told us to back off when we wanted to organise a face-to-face with Abram122."

"Yes. You're right. She did, didn't she."

Spence had now taken Harris' idea on board and was prepared to run with it,

"Harris, get that bloodhound nose of yours into her life. Sarah, organise immediate surveillance of her house and get me her car details. The office will have a record of them from when she parked here, and then stand by the phone for my instructions."

"Yes sir. Where are you going?"

"I'm going to pay her a visit, and Chris, you too Hearn, are coming with me."

01:15

Sarah had followed orders, but they hadn't taken long to do, and after a call to her husband to check that all the family were okay, she got back to scrutinising the documents. In the quiet of the office, it gave her time to think. Time to dwell on their mistake, and believed it wasn't all down to Spence, they were a team. They'd all missed it, and why? Because Sophie was their colleague and friend, and they were making emotionally charged decisions. She then started to think about what other mistakes could they have made and began retracing their steps. Nothing seemed to stick out until she wrote down what they had assumed. She knew that was always a hazardous area, but all had panned out to be as expected until she looked at the report on Chris' and Jake's visit to the house. What had they assumed? They assumed Sophie had arrived home from work. They assumed that when they picked her car up on CCTV, it had been taken from her house. What if she never arrived home? Sarah decided to investigate. Firstly, she would check the station CCTV to check that she'd left when they assumed she did. Secondly, she would ask Geoff to follow the car's journey on CCTV.

Meanwhile, Spence had arrived at Brenda Watson's house to find it unoccupied and no car in the drive. The surveillance team reported that no activity had taken place since they arrived at 00:30. They were ordered to remain in place until further notice.

Harris had been successful in his search and found out that she had divorced her husband of fifteen years, an Irish banker, in two thousand and fourteen. The acrimonious split following the disclosure of his involvement in a three-million-pound fraud. He is presently three years into a ten-year sentence at Mountjoy prison in Dublin. She has no children of her own but did foster children between 1992 and 2009. He was unable to find their names due to confidentiality rules and has made an official request for the information. Under the circumstances, they assured him that they would progress the request ASAP.

Back in the IT room, Sophie was identified as leaving the station car park at 00:29 Wednesday 19th December. Geoff had followed the car zipping from one camera to another until she failed to appear on the consecutive camera in the series. It could mean that she decided to leave the main road and perhaps knew a shortcut through side roads, but at that time in the morning, traffic was light, and there would be little point. Sarah pulled up a map of the section in question. Together with Harris, who had brought them both a cuppa, scoured the streets for anywhere that she may have gone. It couldn't have been to visit Brenda Watson because she lived a good twenty minutes away, in a different direction.

"Hang on." said Harris, "Look. This must be an old map because of that spot there." Pointing to a large plot beside the main road. "That is now a McDonald's."

"Are you sure?"

"Absolutely, I stopped for a Big Mac only last week."

"They'll have cameras, won't they?"

Harris nodded, "Yep. Let's go."

Sarah asked Geoff to keep looking at the CCTV while they were away, in case she turned up later, or even further down the road.

When they arrived, both were surprised at how busy the place was. You'd think it could be six in the evening. Harris commented that the lack of kids would be the giveaway, and Sarah had to agree. In the main, they were nightclubbers and partygoers on their way home. Sarah asked to see the manager, while Harris examined the menu,

Sarah nudged his arm, "Don't even think about it."

Almost immediately, a young man who looked almost too young to be out on his own, came around the counter. Sarah explained that they were tracking a missing person and would appreciate his help. And although he was a tender age, his professionalism rang out, and in a matter of minutes, they were seated in his office viewing the CCTV.

They identified Sophie's car entering the car park at 00:38. She parked and was seen entering the restaurant. They were now able to switch to the internal cameras and watched as she ordered a drink and sat at a table in the window. She sat alone for five minutes until being joined by another woman. Harris asked if they could zoom in. The manager said it wouldn't make any difference because the person's back was towards them, and suggested viewing from a different camera, at a better angle, and there she was, Brenda Watson.

At that moment Sarah's phone rang. It was Chris informing them that Sophie's phone records had finally arrived, and the last person she spoke to was… he didn't manage to complete his sentence,

Sarah said it for him, "Brenda Watson!"

Harris and Sarah continued to watch the CCTV. It was about fifteen minutes later that Sophie left the restaurant. Brenda remained in her seat. Were they wrong about her? Blimey! One step forward and two steps back. They changed to the external camera and watched intently as Sophie walked to her car. She had her keys in her hand and was about to put the key in the lock when two men approached. One must have asked her the time because she pulled her sleeve back to check her watch, and in a split second, the keys were snatched from her hand, she was bundled into the back seat of her car and the mini then sped away. Sarah was immediately on the phone with Geoff, gave him the time and asked him to track her car. He said he'd already seen her leave and had tried to track it, but it had pulled off into a side road and who knows where it went then. Sarah knew that to trace it through side streets would require a massive operation to be mounted, with feet on the ground searching for cameras. They didn't have time for that, Sophie wouldn't survive for that long. They would now have to focus their attention on Brenda and hope she could lead them to Sophie, but Geoff told them that her car too had left the main road and he was unable to trace it.

Twenty-One

Thursday 20th December – 01:50

Sophie had managed to retrieve her clothing and although the restraint prevented her from putting them on, she could at least, cover herself up. It was a meagre comfort in her hell because her predicament remained the same. She was still held at the mercy of Duffy, and the prospect of being raped when the men returned, was very real.

It was now that the cold had started to bite and so too did the pain in her ankle. She'd been tied up for so long, that it had become sore, and uncomfortable. Reaching down to massage it, she noticed that something had changed. She could get a finger under the rope. A glimmer of hope rose in her heart. Could it be that in his hurry to leave the barn, the moron hadn't tied it up properly? And for the first time, she allowed herself a smile. Although her ankle was swollen and sore, she gritted her teeth and worked through the pain to push the rope down the back of her heel. Bit by bit it moved further down until all of a sudden, it slipped underneath, and the rope was off. As she got to her feet, the pain of freedom was intense, her ankle couldn't take any weight, and the throb of blood returning was so severe, that she bit on her hand to stifle a scream.

She scrambled to get dressed, and that made her feel a lot better and less vulnerable. Although her experience at the hands of the two men, would not be as easily remedied. Images of their faces, their depraved expressions as they leered at, and touched her naked parts, would be the stuff of nightmares and left her feeling violated, humiliated, ashamed, and permanently nauseous.

In order to survive this ordeal, her thoughts must now turn to escape. She must find an inner strength that she never knew she possessed. Freedom would only be possible if she could find a way out. And to that end, hobbled past the hay bales to the side of the barn, and began feeling for weakened planks that she could squeeze through. At this point, she didn't have a plan B, but one was soon to present itself.

Duffy had opened the barn door. There was a lot of shuffling and cursing, as he seemed to stumble about. Sophie hid behind the hay bales waiting for the shout when he realised that she was no longer restrained. It wasn't immediately forthcoming, and the wait for the inevitable sent her pulse racing. She decided to take a couple of steps to the right, where she could peep around the bale to see what was happening.

She couldn't see Duffy, but she could hear him. He was cursing as he dragged something along, first over gravel, then over concrete. He was bringing something into the barn. And that something was a large petrol can. She moved further to the right to get a better view, and there they were, four large cans of petrol lined up against the upright timbers. It was now that she realised what he had planned for her, and her blood ran cold.

Twenty-Two

Thursday 20th December – 03:00

Everyone had now returned to the station and sat together in Spence's office, and everyone was in the same mindset, to continue for as long as it takes.

"We're getting close folks; we just need that final push over the line. Any suggestions anyone?"

They all seemed just as wanting. Frustration etched on every face. Sarah hoped that the APW she'd issued for Brenda's car would reap rewards soon, but in the meantime, she would resume with the invoices where she left off, placing those she'd checked into neat piles on the floor. But something made her stop what she was doing. Something had caught her attention.

"What is it Sarah?" asked Spence.

"Why would you have two electric bills for the same quarter?"

"You wouldn't."

She reached down, picked them both up, and laid them side by side on the table,

Harris craned his head to see, "They're for different addresses but both invoiced to Duffy."

"What are the addresses?"

Sarah said one was his house in Brixton, and the other was an address in the East Grinstead area, and handed the bill over to Chris who was already opening Google maps. He identified the property,

"It's very isolated, it will be difficult to approach without being seen." And turned the monitor for all to see.

Spence began his trademark pacing,

"We need some evidence before we run with this," he announced. "Jake, call the local boys and ask them to initiate urgent surveillance, I need to know if there are any vehicles on that property. Sarah, get on to DCI Fielding, inform him of our news and ask him to sanction and ready armed response. And all of you, get your kit on and be ready to move. If it's confirmed that a white Mercedes is on site, then we go in thirty minutes. Jake, call me as soon as you know, I'll be in the cells talking to Sammi Mancini, she might know something about the place."

It was now Chris' turn to pace. Waiting for that call was torture, his mind full of the worst type of thoughts; images of Sophie being beaten or falling victim to the needle. Indeed, everyone would have been fearing the same but to Chris, Sophie was more than a colleague, she was special to him, and he was planning to move their relationship forward when this was all over. At last, a call, Jake pounced on the phone,

"The Mercedes is confirmed!" he shouted. And phoned Spence who got the call as he was leaving the cells following his chat.

It appeared that a few hours of police hospitality had not been a good experience for Sammi, and she was now willing to cooperate. She confirmed that Duffy rented the East Grinstead property, and then dropped the bombshell, that Brenda Watson owned it and was Duffy's foster mother. With a call to DCS Black, the order to go was approved, and the operation sprang into life.

DI Bennett and DSU Merriman were to coordinate and monitor the action from the CID office. The extent of the operation preparedness confined to hurried conversations in passageways and stairwells - the meat for the bare bones plan to be drip fed on route.

In the station car park, a fleet of squad cars had begun to

leave the compound. Two by two, they staggered their exit and made their way to designated positions close to the property. Fielding, having elected to join the troops, was riding in an unmarked car with Spence, Chris Sparkes and Harris. Sarah, Hearn, and Jake were in another.

On the road, the meat on the bone was coming in. The police helicopter, equipped with thermal sensors, reported observing one person in the courtyard of the property moving about freely and confirmed a stationary heat source in the barn.

On hearing the news, Chris rallied from his morose mood, "That has to be Sophie!"

The others remained quiet, hoping he was right, but not wanting to commit themselves.

"If it's heat, then the person must be alive," concluded Spence. "Let's hope it's our Sophie."

And in a matter of minutes came more news, just what they were waiting for, that Brenda Watson's car had been picked up on ANPR leaving Croydon,

"She's on her way to East Grinstead," said Fielding. "Tell them not to make a stop, to keep her under surveillance and to keep a good distance." Being mindful that the only card they were holding, was the element of surprise. They couldn't risk Brenda realising that eyes were on her, she might call ahead and tip them off, and if Sophie was still alive, she wouldn't be for much longer.

03:30

Brenda was completely unaware of the attention. Unaware that the connection had been made between her and Duffy, and was on her way to the farmhouse, in total ignorance of what will take place when she arrives.

Her plan was to speak to Sophie, to apologise for her son's

behaviour and to ask for her forgiveness, believing that when the barn is torched, that she would have made her peace with Sophie before her death.

Of course, she had to die, she didn't want her to, she liked her, but it was either her or her son. And the thought of that made her angry. Angry with herself for not dealing with her son long before it got to this stage. She knew of his predilections, of course she did, but as a doting mother, was incapable of preventing him from indulging in his sexual and sadistic hobby.

She had taken the fourteen-year-old boy into her home as a foster child when his birth mother died. The term, mother, being up for debate in this case. Although, they could never get him to talk about it, evidence acquired by the professionals confirmed he had been sexually abused by her, and subject to abuse by the many male clients that visited the home on a daily, or perhaps even hourly basis. Not surprising then, that his father was never known, and Duffy grew up with a warped and perverted view of life and love.

From the outset, Brenda and Duffy had a strong bond, stronger than she ever had with any of the other children, and it wasn't long before he began calling her mum, and she coveted him as if she was his true mother. She idolised him, cared for him, loved him, indulged him, and protected him. Although at times he could be a naughty boy, he always managed to talk her around to his way of thinking. Until recently that is, when she found out about his new unhealthy hobby. He'd kept her in the dark about that, and she wasn't happy about it. She liked dogs and thought he did too, so why watch them kill each other? She didn't understand it but was too weak to stop it. It seems that whatever her son wants, he gets.

He had, however, been more forthcoming about his perceived relationship with Gemma. She knew he had feelings for her. She also knew that he was delusional, that there was no way this young girl would feel the same about him and wasn't surprised when it ended badly.

Of course, she had led him on, it couldn't possibly be that he would have been in the wrong. In her opinion, she was a temptress, a slut, and considered Gemma's videos as carefully choreographed performances, obviously choosing to ignore her son's explicit instructions, commentary, and encouragement. Did she really believe that the fear in her eyes, that the tears which flowed down her cheeks, and the tremble in her hands as she performed for the camera, was all an act? Of course she did because she'd seen it before. And then, just as now, she chose to lay the blame squarely at the feet of the abused. The fact that her son was a sexual pervert, a monster, and a danger to young girls would never cross her mind. For her, it was something he enjoyed, and after all, what harm could it do?

But Gemma was different to the others, he couldn't resign her to memory, she had captured his heart, just as Samantha had done many years before. He believed he loved her and that she would love him too. He must have forgotten that he was now many years older, but it would seem, not any wiser. But Gemma was repelled by him, and that broke his heart. And if he couldn't have her, then no one would.

That fateful night, he'd planned to reveal himself to her; to put a face to the voice that had harried her for the past six months. In his warped mind, his expectation that she would be overjoyed to see him, an understandable belief for a man whose moral compass was woefully misaligned.

Being a meticulous individual, he'd planned everything down to the nth degree. Samantha was out of the way, packed off to Scotland to visit family. A trip he'd organised some weeks before and knew she wouldn't be back until Monday. By then he would have moved Gemma in and packed

Samantha's bags. Her time with him would be over. It would be Gemma's turn to experience his attention, his unique and perverted ways, and he in turn, would again experience the days of his youth.

Sean was ordered to pick Gemma up from Darcy. He refused at first. He liked her and was enjoying the sex she so freely agreed to, naively believing it was love, and he wasn't about to rock the boat, was he? He didn't have to work for it, it was there for the taking, and he wasn't good at sharing. But the promise of a bag filled to the brim with drugs quickly turned his head, and Gemma, who was totally besotted with Sean, never thought to question the reason for the weekend and blindly walked into the arms of the devil.

All was going to plan. Between them they'd demolished the pizza delivered an hour before, ordered and paid for by Duffy, and had romped around the house taking selfies, finally resorting to rolling about in the deep pile carpet, when the doorbell rang. Sean left Gemma swimming in the carpet to open it and a few seconds later Duffy entered the room. Gemma was embarrassed and got to her feet. She was looking for a reaction from Sean, but he kept his head down. It was now that Duffy gave the nod for Sean to leave. Gemma assuming they'd both been rumbled by the owner, scooped up her trainers and walked towards the door. Duffy put an arm out to stop her. She was confused and called out for Sean. He didn't reply. She called again, and still no reply.

Duffy who had now taken off his jacket and thrown it down on the sofa, made no comment. He stood with hands on hips, undressing her with his eyes. Little by little he moved down her body, wetting his lips with his tongue as if about to devour her. His breathing quickened and grew louder. All her instincts told her to run, but Duffy stood between her and the door. She screamed out for Sean to take her with him, but he'd long gone. His job was done, and he was now on his way to visit Jasmine, who in the passage of time would also test positive for Chlamydia.

Mesmerised by her heaving breast that he'd longed to fondle, Duffy made his move, grabbing the collar of her blouse and undoing the buttons. She tried to push him away, but he was too strong and determined to feel the flesh inside her blouse. It was now that she began to cry. He wasn't deterred, he was used to her tears, and he liked it; it made him feel powerful. He pulled her towards him and whispered in her ear,

"My sweetheart, it's me, you're safe now."

Her blood ran cold. It was the voice of the shepherd. The voice of the man who had abused and degraded her. The man who had made her life a misery. Her shoulders dropped in despair, she felt sick, grabbed her stomach, and began to whimper. Needless to say, he wasn't impressed by her reaction. It wasn't what he imagined and expected. It made him furious. With one hand he held tight the collar of her shirt, the other he clenched into a fist. The deep grimace on his face showing a man struggling to control his emotions. Was he going to lash out at her? She thought he would, and closed her eyes, cowering in the expectation of a punch in the face. He wanted to hit her but must have thought better of it, and took a step back, as he did his hand slid down over her breast and across her nipple. She shuddered, reviled by his touch, and that was enough for him to erupt into a rage. Red faced and shaking with anger, he bellowed,

"You little bitch! After everything I've done for you!" And lunged at her, grabbed her arm, and dragged her out of the room to the bottom of the stairs, where her legs turned to jelly, and she fell to the floor.

She looked a pathetic soul pulling on his trouser leg, pleading with him to let her go. He gave a salacious smile, tightened his grip on her arm and continued dragging her up the stairs. Petrified, she stumbled from one stair to the next, along the passageway, and into his bedroom where he ordered her to undress. Sobbing and terrified of what he would do if she refused, she complied.

Slowly and tentatively, she peeled off her clothes, trying to delay the inevitable which she assumed would be to carry out her usual performance for him, but that wasn't his plan. He'd had enough of watching.

He too was now naked from the waist down and erect. He ordered her onto the bed. First he tied her hands to the headboard with tie-wraps, then straddled her, his heavy body crushing down on her stomach. She was trapped, unable to move, and barely able to breathe. For a moment he glared at her, any desire he once had for this ungrateful wretch was now dead, replaced by the need for retribution. In the last minutes of her life, he would treat her body as little more than a carcass for the use of, pushing and thrusting inside her until he killed her spirit. She could do nothing to stop him. And when he'd finished with her, and his needs had been met, did he make the decision that she would pay for rejecting him. And she did. With her life.

Fielding was in conversation with the DCI organising the surveillance of the farmhouse. He had been informed of developments and their belief that Sophie might be the person in the barn. It was therefore decided, because it would be getting light soon, to send in armed officers on foot while they could still approach under the cover of darkness.

As they deployed, the shout came that Brenda was in the area and was heading to the lane. The officers took up positions deep within the hedgerows and waited for her to pass.

She pulled up in the drive. Officers watched as she walked up to the house and entered through the front door.

"Ryan!" she called. "Ryan, it's me."

Fielding and his team had now arrived and made a slow, silent approach to within two hundred yards of the property, where they abandoned their vehicles and travelled the rest of the way on foot, meeting up with officers already surrounding the property. They were in position and ready to go on command, but the order couldn't be given until Duffy was located. The helicopter, having been ordered to keep clear of the site, for fear that Duffy would panic if he heard and saw them, and kill Sophie, meant that the troops were in the dark as to his whereabouts on the property.

Meanwhile, Sophie had made her way around the hay bales to a position where she was within five metres of the doorway. She wanted to try and run for it but didn't know if it was closed or locked, and fear of the consequences, should it be locked, was making her decision difficult to make. There was no way she wanted to stay and be burnt to a crisp but finding the courage to make her bid for freedom, taking the risk of being shot or stabbed, was just as frightening.

Her pulse was racing. She was panicking and hyperventilating. Terrified that she might give herself away, she began to withdraw back behind the bale. She took a deep breath and was counting to ten to calm herself down. Slowly she put one foot behind the other, but her legs were weak and trembling. She stumbled and fell to the floor. Gripped with fear, she held on to the bale and slowly wrenched herself up. One more big effort and she would be upright. And just as she got to her feet, Duffy rounded on her and landed an almighty punch in the middle of her back, sending her crashing back to the floor. He wasn't stupid. He knew she'd slipped her rope, and he also knew that she couldn't get far, and decided to finish the job at hand first before going after her. She didn't have a chance.

She struggled but his grip was firm, her feet barely touching the ground as he marched her back to the rope. She pleaded with him to let her go. He wasn't affected. This cold-hearted murderer couldn't care less about her.

The officers had now pushed forward. Chris and Jake had inched their way through the woodland boundary and were squatting behind the barn. Chris could hear Sophie's distressing and despairing pleas. Desperate to go in and save her, he'd succumbed to the red mist and started to make his move, but Jake held him back.

"You go in now, when we don't know what he's up to, you're risking her life."

Brenda had given up looking for her son in the house and had now walked over to the barn. As the door opened, Duffy put a hand over Sophie's mouth and pulled out a knife he had tucked inside his shirt.

"Ryan, are you in here?"

On recognising it was his mother, he put the knife back, pushed Sophie's head away as if he was discarding a piece of rubbish, and walked out to meet her.

"You're late," he whinged. "I wanted to set this off hours ago, it will be light soon."

Brenda tutted, "It doesn't matter when you do it, does it. A fire can start at any time. In fact, a fire during the daytime is more believable." Then looked around. "Where are the boys?"

"They've taken the dogs back." He glanced at his watch, "They should have been back by now."

Sophie, although unable to discern the conversation, had recognised Brenda's voice, her spirits rose, and tears of relief flowed down her cheeks, she thought she was about to be saved. Any second now and she would be released from her hell, but as the seconds ticked away, so too did her patience,

"I'm over here!" she shouted. "Here, by the pit. Brenda, over here!"

There was a moment of activity and then Brenda appeared from behind the hay bales,

She walked over to Sophie and smiled down at her. Sophie, experiencing immense relief, gave a broad and thankful smile back,

"Oh thank God Brenda! I was beginning to think I would die here."

Brenda continued to smile, "I hope my boys have treated you well."

It took a moment for Sophie to digest the comment before she asked, "Your boys?"

And now realised that her expectation of freedom was over. Brenda was revealed as a member of the gang that abducted her. She was devastated. Her soul had been bludgeoned, and her body limp with exhaustion left her powerless and at the mercy of these monsters. And this woman in particular, the person she'd trusted with her most personal thoughts, the one who was supposed to help and support her, was now ready to watch her burn to death, and it seemed there was nothing she could do about it. Her fate was sealed, and the betrayal with the helplessness she experienced as a result of it, made her furious,

"Your boys are fucking morons, rapists, and shit human beings! And so are you, you perverted bitch!" She was distraught, and now struggling to breathe. It was the desperate look of confusion that prompted a response from Brenda,

"My boy, you were going to give him up. I couldn't let you give him away. I couldn't have that."

Sophie who had regained a small measure of control, wiped away the tears with the back of her hand, and shouted out, "I think you're insane! I had no idea who he was!"

Brenda looked over her glasses. She didn't believe her, and wagged her finger,

"I saw his card in your bag."

Sophie remained confused. Her blank expression irritated Brenda,

"You remember! When you dropped it on the floor, and all the contents spilled out."

Sophie recalled the event, "But I don't understand! What card?"

"Now you're taking me for an idiot! I expect you were waiting for your moment, weren't you?" Her face contorted with anger. "Looking for the glory when you'd caught him single-handed. A poke in the eye for the male officers I expect!"

Then leant down, opened her bag, pulled a card out and waved it in front of Sophie. It was a card for the kennels. It had Duffy's name on it, and she now remembered why she had one. Her friend Sally wanted a Jack Russell and had asked her to find out if the kennels had any history with the police. She didn't want to buy a pup from one of those puppy farms. Sophie had said she would ask for her. The friend was just doing her due diligence, and Sophie hadn't given it a second thought when she agreed to help.

Brenda had now made an attempt to get up from the wall but stumbled, and it was now that Sophie saw her chance and found the strength to grab her arm and pull her down onto the floor, where she put her into a choke hold with one arm and held the metal wire to her neck with the other. Brenda didn't know what it was, only that it was sharp and assumed it was a knife. Duffy heard the scuffle and came over,

He towered over Sophie. In his hands he held a scythe aloft, threatening to bring it down on her,

"Let my mother go, you bitch, or I'll take your fucking

head off!" he roared.

Sophie was terrified but couldn't back down. Not now, she had to follow it through and held on tightly to Brenda. If he decided to bring it down on her, he would take his mother's head off too.

"I'm going to die anyway," she shrieked. "So it might as well be now! But your mum is coming with me!"

He threw the scythe down and attempted to lunge at her, but Sophie leant back to avoid him, all the time pushing harder on the wire, and screeched,

"You come near me, and I will rip her throat open!"

He then grabbed at Brenda's arm to try and pull her away, but Sophie pushed even harder on the wire. It pierced the skin, and Brenda screamed. Blood began to trickle down her front, and now it was her turn to look death in the eye, paralysed with fear and losing control of her bladder, she cried out,

"Stop Ryan! Stop! She's going to kill me! Stop please!"

Duffy backed off. His bloodshot eyes full of hatred and anger. He was enraged at his inability to free his mother, picked up the scythe and threw it across the barn, where it embedded itself in a wooden upright.

Spence was now inching his way around the front of the barn along with Harris and Sarah, they heard what was going on, and so too Chris and Jake who were making their way around from the other direction. It was now that one of the armed officer's radios burst into life. They all remained still, hoping that Duffy hadn't heard it, but he had. He now knew that the police were outside and ran to stand by the petrol cans. From his pocket, he took a lighter. Spence and Harris unaware of the plan to torch the barn had made the decision to run in, and on seeing him standing beside the cans with a lighter in his hand, were stopped dead in their tracks.

Duffy taunted them with it, "You come near me, and we all die."

Brenda called out, "Ryan, put it down. Please don't do it son, put it down."

Spence raised his hands, "Duffy, this is not the way to end this. Listen to your mother. Please man, don't do it. There's a trained marksman aiming at you. You don't want to die. Put the lighter down."

All the time, trying desperately to get eye contact, but Duffy's eyes were focused on the lighter, he wasn't listening, his intention was clear. He wasn't going to spend the rest of his life in prison, and as he pressed the lighter to produce a flame, a shot rang out, and he fell like a stone to the floor. Spence kicked the lighter away, and Harris, followed quickly by Sarah, ran to Sophie's aid.

Brenda was hysterical as they pulled her away. Her son was dead. And now released from Sophie's grip, the harrowing screams for her son, as she grappled with them in an attempt to crawl across the floor to reach him, clawed at the core of all who heard it. Her effort, however, was in vain. Two uniformed officers wrestled her to her feet and led her away. This was one lady, regardless of her grief, who would not be afforded any privileges or special treatment. Her screams could still be heard as they marched her across the gravel and secured her in a waiting squad car.

Sophie, now released from the rope, quietly wept in relief. Her ordeal was over. For Spence, his next move was to get everyone out of the barn. Nobody knew what Duffy had planned, there could well be other deadly surprises in store.

Fielding was in the courtyard organising the operation and coordinating the movement of personnel, away from the barn and back to the safety of the lane. Specialist firefighters were now on site and ready to take over. Their job was to ensure the scene was safe before officers would be allowed back in to conduct their search.

Chris had asked to walk with Sophie to the ambulance. He was desperate to console her, desperate to wrap his arms around her, but she flinched at his touch, and pulled away. She didn't want the attention and made a point to avoid physical contact with everyone, even Sarah. Silently and mournfully, she sat alone on the ambulance bed, with a silver blanket wrapped tightly around her. Her head lowered, almost tucked inside it, obscuring her face, obscuring her humiliation, and obscuring her agony.

Twenty-Three

Friday 21st December – 08:00

It had been a full twenty-four hours since the team returned to the station following the raid. Essential reporting and debriefing had taken a further chunk of time, but nevertheless, they'd all managed to get some sleep before the next shift.

Refreshed, revitalised, and wiser from their experience, they rolled up ready for another day at the office. Sarah had walked straight into a marital dispute that turned nasty, so barely had time for a coffee before getting back in the car on route to the hospital. Harris was working with Fiona, and in his element, identifying and tracking down the girls on Duffy's laptop, and Chris had been partnered with Hearn to investigate a builder from Croydon, suspected of murdering his girlfriend.

Jake was an absentee. He'd been approached to work on a special operation with the drug squad, they were obviously pleased with his previous performance, and he jumped at the chance. It would be an opportunity to work his way back up the ladder and regain his rank of Detective Inspector. Spence approved it of course, their relationship was back on track, and he wished him every success.

The only detective that failed to sign in would be Sophie, and doctor's orders dictated that she will not be signing in again for some weeks to come.

Fielding had popped in momentarily at the start of the shift, to perform his usual little thank you speech, then with Spence in tow, made their way to a meeting with DCS Black and DSU Merriman. It was understood to be an opportunity for the officers in charge of the Williams and Duffy cases, to update their seniors. No doubt Black and Merriman will be facing the cameras soon, and neither of them would want to be stuck for answers.

Fielding was buoyant and upbeat, informing the group with his usual verve, that Williams will be answering a litany of charges. Jubilantly and proudly he read them out, concluding that his man will no longer supply and distribute drugs, no longer be able to weaponize goons and send them out to terrorise people, and no longer have the means or opportunity to maim and murder.

Spence was less demonstrative. It may have been because he was tired, or more likely because another one of his female officers found herself in a dire situation. Fortunately, she survived, but the responsibility for her predicament lay heavily on his shoulders. For him, the operation had been successful, but it came at a huge cost and could find no reason to celebrate.

He would start by telling the group that Sammi Mancini would not be charged in connection with Sophie's abduction or Gemma's and Sean's murder. She would, however, be charged with perverting the course of justice, and remain under investigation concerning the supply of drugs to the teenagers in her care.

With regards to Gemma's murder, Brenda Watson has confirmed that Dr Ryan Duffy killed her with a lethal injection of Fentanyl, and that she had informed him of her mental state, which ultimately led to his decision to leave her on the train tracks. The expectation was that people would assume she had committed suicide. What neither of them anticipated, was that his stepbrothers, Gerry, and Connor Brady, would panic and run off, leaving her beside the track, instead of on it.

She also confirmed that the warden, James Wilson, had seen Gemma's dead body in the storeroom, thought it was

John Taylor who had killed her and tried a bit of blackmail. John Taylor,

then went running to Duffy who on hearing the warden had seen the body, and probably knew about her removal too, sent his brothers to deal with him. Both are being charged with his murder, and for their part in the murder of Gemma.

"So, I'm assuming Brenda Watson will not walk our streets for a while either," said Black.

"Absolutely not. She'll be away for a very long time."

"And what about our girl Sophie? How is she?"

"She's with her family in Dorset for a while, but it's early days in her recovery."

"That's quite an ordeal to get over. Do you think she will?"

"I think that girl is tough and determined. She'll have the support of all the team, and we'll make sure she's okay."

"So, all we have left to hear about is Sean McKinney," remarked Merriman. "What did that young kid do to end up dead?"

"We think it was Sean driving the Mercedes, and who picked Gemma up from Darcy, under the pretence that she was spending the weekend with him. But it was Duffy's bed she ended up in, and Duffy's bed she died in. So, in the end, the kid just knew too much."

"Ah, knowledge," declared Black. "Thomas Huxley once said, if a little knowledge is dangerous, where is the man who has so much as to be out of danger?"

"We can't win either way then can we?" suggested Spence.

"But we must keep winning Jack, mustn't we."

They all agreed, but Spence thought the comment was directed at him, a preamble to the speech where he is told that he's too old and given his marching orders. He wasn't about to wait for that,

"Well, actually I feel that after twenty years…"

Fielding who had an inkling about his concerns,

interrupted, "After twenty years you've got knowledge pouring out of your ears, and there's a lot more winning to take place under your command."

Merriman glanced over to Black, then back to Spence, "I hope you weren't about to give us the heave-ho in favour of putting your feet up!"

Expecting the opposite to be suggested, Spence was taken aback, and hesitated before answering, "No sir."

"Well, thank goodness for that," said Black. "We have a great team at this station, and that's how I want it to stay. You've got a few more years in you yet."

Merriman spoke up, "No thoughts of going for DCI then Jack?"

Spence laughed, "Absolutely not sir. Heights make me dizzy."

Merriman laughed at the comment and had expected a humorous retort. Nobody ever got a straight reply from Jack when it came to questions about promotion.

"Very well. Now, no arguments, it's been agreed, you're taking a holiday."

"But sir?"

"No buts, this has been a tough one. Get yourself home and we'll see you in a week."

Fielding leant over and shook Spence's hand, "Well done mate, enjoy your break."

The meeting now at a close, Fielding and Merriman followed Spence to his office where two men were already making themselves comfortable.

"What's going on?" he demanded. "Who are they?"

Merriman put a hand on his shoulder, "Calm down Jack. That is Detective Inspector John Hamilton, seconded in to replace you while you're away."

"And the other?"

"That's Erling Christensen, an observer from the Danish police force."

"Danish!" exclaimed Spence. "My cousin is married to a Danish guy."

"And?" asked Fielding.

"We went there for Christmas, and they made me eat rice pudding. They're mad about it you know."

Fielding tried to stifle a laugh, but couldn't, "Spence. Seriously, you need a break!"

Spence looked horrified, "I better not get back to find my desk drawers full of bloody rice pudding!"

Merriman and Fielding both found his reaction hilarious,

"Oh, that's made my day," chuckled Merriman. And handed Spence his coat, Fielding following up with his briefcase,

"Home. Now!" They ordered.

Spence took his case, threw his coat over his shoulder, and left the office muttering.

Merriman turned to Fielding, "What did he say?"

"He said, he bloody hates rice pudding!"

Acknowledgements

A massive thank you to Ben, my ever-patient husband, whose support is unwavering and priceless.

To my grandchildren: Harriet, Anna, Madelyn, Libby, Mikey, Mila, and Marnie for just being themselves, making me smile, and keeping me sane when the writing became challenging.

To my daughters: Sarah and Sophie, my sons: David, Michael and Jack, and my daughters-in-law: Jasmine and Samantha. All were constantly subjected to requests for them to stop what they were doing and to listen to this - does it sound okay? Or read this and get back to me please. Thank you all for your suggestions – I really did listen and it made all the difference.

To my brother-in-law John, and son-in-law Erling for their support and encouragement. And a big thank you to my brother Ron and sister Brenda, their positive and enthusiastic comments subsequently sending me off to the publishers.

I love you all.

Finally, I want to thank Keith at Michael Terence Publishing for giving me the opportunity to publish, and to Karolina for designing such a wonderful, eye-catching cover.

Available worldwide from Amazon
and all good bookstores

www.mtp.agency

Milton Keynes UK
Ingram Content Group UK Ltd.
UKHW021044181223
434584UK00005B/553